Montgomery Lake High #1

Montgomery Lake High #1
The Right Person

Stacy A. Padula

Eloquent Books
Durham, Connecticut

Strategic Book Publishing and Rights Co.
USA | Singapore
www.sbpra.com

For information about special discounts for bulk purchases, please contact Strategic Book Publishing and Rights Co. Special Sales, at bookorder@sbpra.net

ISBN: 978-1-60911-472-5

Book Design by Julius Kiskis

23 22 21 22 20 19 18 17 16   2 3 4 5 6

Dedication

This book is dedicated in loving memory to
Glenn Fredette and Joseph Mattes.

Contents

Prologue

Chris Dunkin

Just shy of my fifteenth birthday, I came to terms with the fact that I was a teenage alcoholic with a pretty serious drug problem. As you can presume, I was traveling fast down the road to destruction. This story my friends and I are about to tell you is important because living it, I learned the true value of my life. It's somewhat of a teenage love story—packed tightly, of course, with all the unimportant drama you'd expect from high school freshmen—but more importantly it is a story of trial, inspiration, revelation, and death.

I'm asking you now to consider the possibility of death shining in a positive light. It's hard to imagine, I know; but as the truth unravels before your eyes (as it did before my own), you will see how experiencing death is the only chance we have of living. I ask you to read with an open mind. You will soon be in the shoes of high school freshmen, when every small bump in the road seems life jeopardizing. Perhaps you're yet to be there, or perhaps you've already been; either way, you must understand most importantly that this is a story about the greatest love of all. The pessimists may say it is impossible for a teenager to comprehend the depth of such love. I believe it is impossible for anyone of any age to comprehend, and I tell you this comfortably from an optimistic point of view.

Love bears all things,
believes all things,
hopes all things,
and endures all things.

one

The world stopped turning, the waves stopped crashing, and the fire stopped dancing as Chris Dunkin laid his eyes on her. He blinked, realizing somehow his life had just been changed. She had arrived at Saquish Beach with her boyfriend and taken a seat across the bonfire. Through the smoke of the fire, Chris studied the girl, attempting to understand why his stomach had lunged into flutters. Her dark hair was pulled back into a loose ponytail with a few stray locks framing her makeup-less face. She wore a gray hooded sweatshirt, a jean skirt, and white flip-flops—similar to what every girl at the party wore. From across the fire, there seemed to be nothing extraordinary about her physical appearance.

Jason Davids nudged Chris and then nodded towards the girl. "Courtney's hot, huh?" he said with wide eyes.

"She's all right," Chris replied, locking his eyes again on the girl Jason had called Courtney.

"That's Mayor Angeletti's daughter," Jason said. "She's more than all right, dude! I'd capitalize on her in a second if she weren't dating Sartelli. Now we know why he kept her hidden for so long."

Chris' eyes traveled to Bryan Sartelli, who was sitting

on the log beside Courtney. Bryan was a good friend of Chris', one whom he valued highly. As Chris' eyes shot back to Courtney's face, he began wondering if his mind were playing tricks on him. How could the sight of someone he'd never met floor him? Were his palms suddenly sweating profusely because of the heat from the nearby fire? Why was his heart pounding so heavily against his muscular chest? Would seeing her for the first time have taken such a tight grip on his heart if he hadn't been high? Yes, he believed it would have.

"I need to go talk to her," Chris said, standing up from his seat suddenly.

Jason looked up at Chris in surprise, and then, slowly rose to meet his best friend. "All right, guy. I'll introduce you," he offered, leading Chris over to where Courtney was seated.

She looked up and smiled at Jason as he appeared before her. It was then that Chris noticed the sparkle in her sky blue eyes. Studying her face up close, Chris was surprised by how attractive he found her features. From across the fire he had not recognized Courtney's beauty, yet he had still been undeniably drawn to her.

"Hello, Courtney. This is Chris," Jason greeted her. "He's a friend of Bryan's too."

"Yeah, he's the guy we go to when we want to have some fun," Bryan explained to his girlfriend as he stood up to slap hands with Chris and Jason.

"It's nice to meet you," Courtney replied softly, dragging her eyes off of Jason and planting them on Chris.

The flutters returned inside Chris' stomach, and he found himself unable to form any words in return. He smiled, nodded, and then walked past Bryan towards the

Atlantic. It was low tide, and the bonfire was ten yards behind Chris when he sat down on the cool ground. Staring
blankly at the waves crashing fifteen feet in front of him,
Chris took off his sandals and pressed his feet deeply into
the moist sand. A moment later, Courtney appeared beside
him. She also took off her shoes and buried her feet in
the sand. The two of them sat quietly, watching the waves
crash on to shore. At that moment all the stars seemed to
align. Although their time alone only lasted a minute before Bryan and Jason joined them by the shore, for the first
time in his life, Chris felt that he was in the right place at
the right time.

two

(Two months later)

The first bell of her high school career was an hour away from ringing. Courtney Angeletti stood before her mahogany framed full-length mirror, carefully examining her reflection. Her pearly white smile broadened, and her bright aquamarine eyes glistened as she thought of the friends she would soon be with. As Courtney slightly twirled to better view the fit of her maroon suede skirt, a piece of her jet-black hair caught the light and shined like the moon on a dark night. Smoothly she ran her perfectly manicured fingernails through her shoulder length mane. Next she brushed imaginary lint from her designer gray, maroon, and white plaid sweater vest. Beneath her vest, Courtney's extra small white cotton blouse hung without an imperfection, fitting perfectly to her slender figure. The excitement of the day ahead and the glow from inside Courtney's heart pasted a permanent smile on her attractive face.

As Courtney ventured through her Victorian bedroom suite, her white gold jewelry shimmered in all directions. Sunlight poured into her room as she approached the

4

sliding glass doors that led to her private balcony. Sliding one door open, she made way onto the granite balcony. A gentle breeze blew against Courtney's baby soft skin as she glanced out at the town below. She reflected on her summer, the beach, Bryan, the new friends she had made, and her family vacation in the Hamptons. She thought of the first time she met Chris and how much her life had changed as a result. Although she felt guilty for breaking up with Bryan so suddenly, she was trying to ignore the sting in her heart. Two months prior, Chris Dunkin had captivated her.

At first she had thought it had been God prompting her to break up with Bryan for Chris. After getting to know Chris, she was having second thoughts. She had found Bryan somewhat boring, and the idea of dating a party-kid like Chris had sounded exciting. No matter how hard she tried to convince herself that that had been the basis of her decision, she knew it was not the truth. She could not understand the force that had overcome her and moved her to break up with Bryan.

Before dating Chris, Courtney had been very spiritual. Lately, she found herself struggling to make it to church on Sundays, let alone to Youth Group on Fridays. Courtney knew her family was growing concerned for her, but she had somehow managed to block it out. In fact, she was surprised to be thinking about it at all.

Less than a mile away, Marielle Kayne stared into her full-length mirror. Gleaming with excitement, her smile widened as butterflies fluttered around her stomach. She glanced to her manicured fingernails. Painted a shimmering shade of blue, they matched perfectly with her cotton skirt and jacket. On her feet were the new leather shoes she had bought with her best friend, Courtney. The creamy white shoes complimented the sleeveless blouse she wore beneath her jacket. In a half-hour, she would start her first period of high school.

Although Julianna Camen's summer away in New Hampshire had been lonely without her best friends, Courtney and Marielle, Julianna valued the time she had spent with her family. In just a half-hour, she would be reunited with her best friends. Her blue eyes drifted to the frameless mirror that hung on her pastel bedroom wall. She admired the way her soft, dirty blonde hair fell upon her petite shoulders. The purple polo shirt and white shorts she wore not only complimented her slim figure, but also perfectly matched her new cross trainers. Grabbing her white backpack off of her bed, she took one last glance at her reflection.

"My hair is so flat!" Cathy Kagelli complained, rushing to get ready in another house across Montgomery. She glared at herself in the bathroom mirror. *Why on such an important day can I not get my appearance up to standard?* She sighed. *True, my hangover from Chris' party probably isn't helping my case.* "Chantal, where is the hairspray?"

"Under the sink, Cath!" Chantal Kagelli called to her discouraged, identical twin sister.

Chantal was relieved she had not attended Chris' party. Her silky auburn hair neatly fell past her shoulders as the refreshing smell of herbal shampoo twitched her nose. Her suntanned skin complimented her twinkling green eyes and bright white smile.

"Chantal," Cathy moaned, entering Chantal's spacious bedroom, "do you have any aspirin up here? My head feels like it is continuously being smashed between two cars."

"Check the medicine cabinet," Chantal replied, rolling her eyes as she pushed past her sister.

Across town, Mrs. Sartelli hollered down the hallway for the third time that morning: "Bryan, get up!"

"I am," Bryan mumbled, placing his head beneath two pillows. Why was he so tired? Bryan was never this tired. As he started to wake up, flashbacks of Chris' party flooded his mind. *How could my parents let me stay out so late on a school night?* Bryan ruminated, climbing out of his bed. Then, he remembered, *oh yeah, they didn't.* Chris' party had begun at midnight when his parents thought he was asleep—not getting wasted.

"I hate school," Bryan muttered, stumbling to stand up straight. His room spun when he tried to focus on his clock. The numbers blurred together, and he realized that he was still drunk.

"Bryan!" his mother screeched. "I want you down here,

ready, in two minutes!"

Quickly Bryan threw a pair of khaki cargo pants over his flannel boxers. Tripping over one of his brown leather shoes, Bryan reached for a gray T-shirt that hung around his bedpost. He quickly threw on the shirt and shoes and exited his bedroom—once again tripping over something or other.

Jon Anderson, another soon-to-be-freshman at Montgomery Lake High, woke up at seven—thankful he had not been drunk the night before. Although he had attended Chris' party, he had not felt the desire to do anything in which his friends had indulged. His girlfriend, Alyssa, had not been able to sneak out of her house for the party, and Jon was grateful for that. Don't misunderstand—Jon adored Alyssa's presence. She had been his best friend for years before they ever began dating. Jon was happy Alyssa had not attended the party because he hated watching her cave to peer pressure. Although Jon hung out with a crew known for throwing wild parties, doing drugs, and getting into trouble, he liked to think of himself differently. Chris, Jason, and Bryan had been his best friends since their idea of partying was eating Hoodsie Cups.

Jon dressed in his usual attire: a button-up Abercrombie dress shirt, jeans, and shell-toe sneakers. He brushed his teeth, washed his face, and spiked his short blonde hair before heading downstairs to have breakfast with his younger sister and brother. After making them oatmeal, Jon only had time to grab a power bar to eat on the bus. He was fine with that; after staying up until 3:30 a.m., he could definitely use the energy.

In a mansion across Montgomery, Jason Davids had finally fallen asleep around five-thirty that morning. At the
sound of his mother's voice calling him down to breakfast, he shot his large blue eyes wide open. It was seven
o'clock, and Jason could not have felt more awake. Quickly,
he made his way over to the bureau on which he had laid
out his clothing the previous night. He threw on his neatly
ironed khakis and green striped dress shirt, allowing his
shirt hang in front of his pants. Jason was a firm believer
in dressing up for all occasions, even the first day of school.
It probably had something to do with the fact that he had
never seen either of his parents wear jeans. His father was
a lawyer, and his mother was an interior designer, so they
always dressed professionally. Jason, like his parents, was
more comfortable looking good than wearing casual clothing. Before running downstairs to eat breakfast with his
family, Jason looked up at his reflection. Wonderful—his
pupils were back to their normal size.

"Chris, get up!" his younger sister squeaked as she
flicked his bedroom light on and off.

"Turn the light off, Katie!" Chris demanded, moaning as
he stuffed his messy blonde head of hair beneath a pillow.

"Chris, it's the first day of school! You have to go!" Katie
urged. "Come on, Chris," she pleaded, tugging on his muscular arm.

"Ohhhh," he moaned, opening his baby blue eyes.
"What time is it?"

"Seven-twenty," Katie said, glaring at her older brother.

"What's your problem?" Chris questioned her as he rolled out of bed.

"Your friends ate all the food Mom and Dad left for us," Katie responded. "That was our food for the next ten days!"

"Huh?" Chris asked, pulling a light blue American Eagle T-shirt over his head.

"Are you sick?" Katie asked, eyeing her brother curiously.

"Come on, Katie. Let's find something for breakfast," Chris said, avoiding her question. Pulling a pair of khaki shorts over his boxers, he exited his disastrous bedroom. "What happened to the house?" he asked, halting to observe his surroundings.

"Oh, your friends did this too," Katie replied as she descended the cluttered stairs. "You don't remember?"

Chris sighed. "Yeah, now I remember."

"No, you don't!" Katie exclaimed, turning to face her brother. "You never remember anymore, Chris! I saw you last night. Don't think I didn't. I see you all the time, smoking and drinking. You're a mess!"

"You don't know what you see," Chris retorted, tripping over an empty beer ball that lay on the living room floor.

"You're a loser," Katie stated, angrily snatching her book bag from the kitchen counter.

three

Although Courtney was physically seated in homeroom, she was mentally in another place— back at Chris' party, laughing at his foolish antics and socializing with his friends. Recently, Courtney had felt the desire to rebel tug at her heartstrings; at Chris' party, she took her first step in that direction. Although she did not drink any of the alcohol present at the party, she had felt satisfied just being in attendance. Even though Bryan and Chris were part of the same social circle, Bryan had always chosen time with Courtney over the partying scene. Since she began dating Chris, she had become part of their social circle—finally!

Montgomery Lake High was made up of students from all three Montgomery middle schools: Hamilton, Sterling, and Montgomery Lake. Courtney was well acquainted with everyone from Hamilton, where she had been the student body vice president. Additionally, she had accrued ties to the other two middle schools by hanging out with Chris. Chris and his best friend, Jon Anderson, had attended Montgomery Lake. Jason, Chris' other best friend, had studied at a private middle school, but his girlfriend, Cathy Kagelli, had gone to Sterling.

Courtney was in the process of becoming friends with Cathy—a socialite of Chris' crew. Being Chris Dunkin's girlfriend won Courtney favor in the eyes of many, but it didn't seem to win her any points with Cathy. Cathy was beautiful, powerful, and aware that she possessed both attributes. As Jason Davids' girlfriend, Cathy could run the show without much opposition. Courtney was not sure if Cathy liked having another girl in her crew, or if she viewed Courtney as a threat. Courtney didn't want to compete for popularity; she just wanted fun friends.

Courtney felt guilty about avoiding her childhood best friend, Julianna Camen, for the last few weeks; however she had decided that fitting in with Chris' crew should be her first priority. In order to be fully accepted by them, Courtney could not associate with a *goody-goody* like Julianna. Quite frankly, Julianna had nothing in common with Courtney's new friends and very little in common with Courtney—aside from ten years of friendship. Once she began dating Chris, Courtney made a lot of adjustments to her lifestyle. Unfortunately for Julianna, she happened to be one of them.

"Hey, Angeletti!" Jon Anderson yelled from across Courtney's homeroom. Everyone looked up from his or her class schedules except for Courtney. "Court!" Jon exclaimed as he walked over to her desk.

"Huh?" Courtney asked, startled as she came out of her daze. "Oh! Jon, hi."

"Hey," he smiled, taking a seat beside her. "Um, Chris told me to give you this," he said, referring to the note he had just thrown on her desk. "It's nothing bad, so don't worry. Oh, I'll introduce you to Alyssa at lunch. Sorry she couldn't make it last night. I'm looking forward to introducing her to you."

"Can't wait," Courtney said, staring into Jon's rich chocolate eyes. "You look awfully tired. You should go home today and rest. Chris is having another party tomorrow night, so I'm going to sleep all day after school."

"Nah," Jon said and shook his head. "I'm used to no sleep."

———◆———

"JD, my man, waz-up!" Chris Dunkin called out loudly as he entered his homeroom.

"Hey!" Jason Davids greeted him, slapping hands with his best bud. "Nice party last night."

"Did ya like it, Jay?" Chris asked distractedly. "I don't remember it at all. We destroyed my house. It's completely foodless. I feel really bad for Katie," he admitted in a somber tone.

"And you're having another one tomorrow night?" Jason questioned him, eyeing Chris strangely.

"Did I say that?" Chris asked, shaking his head in disgust.

"Yeah, dude, after we killed the last beer ball," Jason laughed, patting Chris on the back. "Wow! You really did have a rough night. Geez!"

"My sister said she saw me at the party," Chris said and glanced at the floor. "I didn't do anything too terrible, did I?"

"You're asking the wrong person!" Jason exclaimed, throwing his muscular arms out in front of him. "I dropped a few tabs with you early last night. I have no freaking clue how I got home this morning. You're always the life of our parties, guy. That's a rep you should want to keep."

Staring blankly at his friend's tired face, Chris reflected upon himself. For the past two years, he had been "the life of the party." Scary—he had no idea that he had tripped the night before. He must have been completely wasted when he agreed to take acid on a school night. Finding out he had mixed acid with alcohol, and God knows what else, explained why Chris had blacked-out. What Katie had said earlier, when Chris was leaving for school, sharply pierced his heart. He absolutely hated the person he had become: a terrible brother, an alcoholic, a user, an emotionally disconnected boyfriend, and a mother's worst nightmare of a son. He had begun to think there could be more to life than partying and getting high. He wanted to escape from his life. He was in over his head. How had he already gotten addicted to alcohol, nicotine, and marijuana? Those were just his addictions, never mind the long list of other drugs he had tried. How had he sunk to that level? Worse, how could he get out? All of these thoughts had been haunting his mind for the last few months.

Chris did not want Courtney to get pulled into his clique. He liked her the way she was: innocent, pure, and full of respectable values. The rumors were true; his friends were ruthless and wild. In fact, Chris was beginning to hate his social life as much as his academic world. That was another problem. In the past year, his grades had dropped from honor roll to Fs. At football camp over the summer, MLH's JV coach told Chris he might want him on the team. That would require Chris to pass all of his classes and periodic drug tests. Ever since peewee football, he knew he had been blessed with a great deal of athletic talent. With football, Katie, and Courtney in mind, he knew it was time to clean up his life.

"Chris, are you with me?" Jason asked, waving his hand before Chris' face.

"Huh?" Chris questioned him, escaping from his daze. "What'd you just say?"

"Tomorrow night, your place again, right?" Jason asked.

Chris shrugged. "I don't think it's a good idea, Jay."

Jason raised his eyebrows and then nodded. "All right man. I'll cover for you," he said, patting his best friend on the shoulder. "You sound like you have some stuff to deal with."

Chris smiled slightly and grabbed the top of his head. He tensely pulled on his short blonde hair. "Thanks, guy," he replied, feeling not at all relieved.

four

itting in his fourth period journalism class, Bryan paid no attention to his teacher. His brown eyes had drifted to the picture of Courtney that he kept in his wallet. Bryan had treated Courtney like the treasure she was, the whole time they were together. What had he done wrong?

As if breaking up with him wasn't hurtful enough, Courtney had made the situation much more painful by immediately dating one of his friends. Bryan had liked Courtney for over a year before they had begun dating. *Chris knew that.* Bryan and Courtney had celebrated their year and a half anniversary right before Courtney broke up with him. Chris knew that too. Bryan had been Chris' friend for close to a decade. *How could Chris see nothing wrong with dating Courtney?* Bryan loved Courtney more than anyone. He hated himself for introducing her to his own best friend.

Bryan couldn't understand why Courtney was attracted to Chris. She was a down-to-earth, honorable, honest, ethical, devout Christian. *Shouldn't Chris look like Satan to someone like her?* Bryan realized that he had many flaws of his own, but Chris' flaws made Bryan's flaws look like virtues.

Courtney swore that Chris had nothing to do with their breakup. She said that ninth grade should be a year for new beginnings. She said that she needed to grow up and, therefore, could not continue dating her middle school boyfriend. Going to out of control parties, trashing people's homes, and experimenting with drugs did not register in Bryan's mind as "growing up." In fact, that was parallel to Bryan's life before he dated Courtney— a lifestyle he had been smart enough to abandon.

"Hi Court," Julianna said, walking over to her during lunch. "Where are we going to sit?"

"Hello," Courtney replied in an unfriendly tone. "I'm going to sit over there," Courtney said, pointing to the lunch table where Chris and his friends were sitting. "If you need help finding a place to sit, I'm sure one of the teachers would be glad to assist you."

Staring at Courtney through pain filled eyes, Julianna struggled to fight back tears. What had she done to offend Courtney? They had been best friends since Kindergarten. "Do you know where Marielle is sitting?" Julianna asked, attempting to show no sign of being hurt.

"Hmmm, I invited her to sit with me," Courtney answered slowly, "but I think she sat with Cathy's twin sister."

Ouch. "Oh, okay," Julianna replied, glancing around the cafeteria as she swallowed the large lump in her throat.

"Whatever," Courtney said with a shrug before hustling across the cafeteria.

After buying her lunch, Marielle walked over to Chantal Kagelli's nearly full lunch table. In homeroom, Chantal had wasted no time introducing herself to Marielle and making her feel comfortable. "Hi," Marielle said as she approached Chantal. "Can I sit here?"

"Sure!" Chantal agreed and smiled warmly.

"I was going to sit with my friend Courtney," Marielle explained as she took a seat, "but I feel uncomfortable around her new friends."

"Don't let them intimidate you," Chantal commented matter-of-factly. "My sister is sitting there with her boyfriend, Jason. I thought of sitting there too, but I can't associate with people like them."

"Who's that Alyssa girl?" Marielle asked, referring to a pretty girl from their homeroom whom she had seen sitting at Courtney's table.

"Alyssa Kelly?" Chantal questioned her and raised her eyebrows. "She was my best friend until she stole my boyfriend. So, as you can guess, we're not really close anymore."

"Who would dump you for her?" Marielle asked, wide eyed.

"Jon," Chantal sighed, pointing to the attractive blonde sitting beside Alyssa. "Except that's not how it happened."

"What do you mean?" Marielle asked, feeling at ease with Chantal.

"It's a long story. I guess it's no secret though. Pretty much everyone from Sterling and Montgomery Lake heard about it." Chantal sighed and bit her bottom lip.

"Oh, sorry to pry. You don't have to tell me," Marielle said quickly, picking up on Chantal's hesitation.

"Oh, it's okay. I just feel bad talking about them," Chantal admitted, "even though it's not really a private thing.

I guess it's better for you to hear it from me than from anyone else. I can only imagine how people twist the story when they tell it. Jon was really popular at his middle school, which I didn't go to, so he had a lot of girls chasing him. He's from Montgomery Lake—so are Alyssa and Chris. Jon and I grew up together in church and eventually started dating. After we'd been going out for a while, I became friendly with Alyssa. She and Jon were wicked close, so she was always around.

"By the time Jon and I had been together for five months, Alyssa had become my best friend. I had no idea that she liked Jon, so I trusted her with everything! Somehow Cathy found out that Alyssa liked Jon, and they began to plot behind my back. One day, while I was at the mall with Alyssa, I think Cathy pretended to be me and broke up with Jon."

Marielle dropped her jaw in disbelief.

"When I got home from Alyssa's, I called Jon," Chantal continued. "He seemed really confused to hear from his ex-girlfriend. I asked him what he was talking about, but he said that he had to go call his new girlfriend—Alyssa!"

"Are you kidding me?" Marielle exclaimed, widening her eyes in horror. "Did you kill them?"

"Well, I haven't really talked to Alyssa lately," Chantal informed her, glancing towards Courtney's lunch table. "The only reason why I talk to Cathy is because we share a bathroom. I am always looking for ways to avoid them both. I don't even know how it all happened. Alyssa claimed that she had nothing to do with it. Cathy not only denied pretending to be me, but also said that Jon and Alyssa had been hooking up behind my back for months. I never even heard Jon's side of the story. It was a disaster."

"I'm sorry you went through all that," Marielle said sympathetically. She did not like what she was hearing about Courtney's new clique. She didn't like it at all.

Meanwhile, Courtney sat down beside Chris at his and his friends' *chosen* lunch table. "Hi, guys," she greeted them. "What's up?"

"Hi, Court," Chris replied, smiling at his perky girlfriend.

"Hey, Court!" Jon called from across the table. "This is Alyssa," he said, referring to the dirty-blonde sitting beside him.

"Hi!" Courtney exclaimed in her usual warm tone. "I'm Courtney, Chris' girlfriend."

"Right," Alyssa replied, looking Courtney up and down. She turned to Cathy Kagelli, who was sitting beside her, and whispered something into her ear. A small laugh escaped from Cathy's mouth, and then she sent a hard to read smile in Courtney's direction.

Courtney was perplexed, but Alyssa smiled at her and explained, "Your sister dates my brother."

"John Kelly is your brother?" Courtney asked, recalling her older sister's long-term boyfriend.

Alyssa nodded. "I thought you would have put that together."

Courtney shook her head. "My sister told me that John had a sister, but she never said more than that. Wow, that's so weird!" Alyssa smiled and turned back towards Cathy.

"Hi, Courtney," a familiar voice called, stealing her attention away from the girls.

"Hi," she replied, turning towards her ex-boyfriend. "How's it going, Bryan?"

"Not too bad," he said and smiled awkwardly. "Hi, Chris."

"Hey," Chris answered lifelessly from the other side of Courtney. "Have fun last night?"

Bryan glared at Chris. Courtney could not blame him. How could Bryan have fun at a party while watching her make-out with Chris the entire time? Knowing how deeply Bryan cared for her, Courtney imagined that the event had felt more like an emotional torture chamber than a party. *Why would Chris ask that question?* Courtney wondered. Chris was a nice person, incapable of intentionally hurting anyone's feelings. Either it was a misunderstanding, or Chris had been too messed up to remember the party.

"Did you?" Bryan retorted.

"I don't know," Chris shrugged. "Did I?" he asked, turning to face Courtney.

Courtney nodded and smiled brightly. "Of course you did! Why else would you have invited everyone back for tomorrow night?"

"Is that what you want?" Chris asked, a hesitant smile spreading across his soft full lips.

Courtney looked at Chris blankly. "Why does it matter what I want?" she questioned him. "It's your house."

Chris smiled at his girlfriend. He appreciated that she failed to take advantage of his offer or his parentless-household. He didn't want to throw another party or even go to one. In fact, he didn't want to hang out with his friends any longer. They would just sink him lower, and Chris knew he was already struggling to keep his head above water.

"I thought you said the party was off?" Jason called from the far end of the table.

"Off?" everyone questioned him in unison.

Chris glanced at his close friends. He realized that, sadly, the only reason they were all friends was their common love of partying. His roots were much deeper with Jason, Jon, and Bryan, but the rest of his friendships were surface at best. "Well I don't know," he responded uneasily, looking down at the table. "Maybe it's . . . it's just . . . I don't want to. . . . I just have to call it off."

"What's with you?" Cathy cried out accusingly. "You've been acting weird ever since you hooked up with Courtney. Did your girlfriend brainwash you or something?" At the sound of Cathy's caustic words, Chris saw Courtney turn bright red.

"Don't bring Courtney into this!" Chris demanded, standing up from his seat. "I don't want to have the party. Maybe I'm sick of having my house trashed and my family mad at me. Can you comprehend that possibility?" Eleven pairs of shock-filled eyes stared back at him.

"Whatever," Cathy said, peeling her calculating eyes off of Chris and placing them upon Courtney. "Maybe you don't want a party, Chris, but Courtney might," she added sweetly.

"Of course she does," Alyssa concluded. "I can tell just by looking at her that she's no low life. Right, Court?"

"Yeah," she agreed, smiling at Alyssa and Cathy. "I like parties."

Chris turned to face Courtney, wondering why she had changed her tune so quickly. Alyssa and Cathy beamed.

"I told you she was just like us," Cathy said loudly.

Alyssa nodded and smiled at Courtney. *Oh God*, Chris thought. *They're working their magic.*

"Listen up, guys. If Chris doesn't have a party tomorrow night, you can count on one at my place," Jason informed everyone at the table. "My parents are going out of town, and they're leaving Matt in charge. Luke has already started throwing out invites. It should be a good time."

"You realize your brother is out of control, don't you?" Alyssa remarked—most likely referring to Luke. "He's going to invite everyone he sees. The entire school is going to show up at your house."

"My night won't be ruined if you stay home." Jason coughed twice and laughed.

Alyssa glared at Jason. "Come on, Courtney," she said, standing up from the rectangular table, "let's go dump our trays."

Courtney immediately stood up and joined Alyssa at the end of the table. She grinned, and Chris assumed she was happy that the girls were being nice to her. Although Chris had been friends with Alyssa for many years, he liked her a lot less than he used to. Before Alyssa became friends with Cathy, she had been a much nicer person. Even though Cathy was dating his best friend, Chris could not bring himself to like her; he thought she was callous and controlling. Courtney was *nothing* like Cathy.

five

"Hi, Mom," Julianna said as she walked through the front door of her home. "How was your day?"

"Hello, Julie," her mother responded from the kitchen. "Come in here. I have a surprise for you."

"Coming," Julianna replied, putting her book bag and binder in the hall closet. A whimper was heard from the kitchen, followed by a loud yip. "A puppy!" Julianna exclaimed, running over to the small Dalmatian. "Oh, Mom, thank you so much! What made you change your mind?"

"Well, your father and I knew that you really wanted one," her mother explained as she sat down at the kitchen table.

"You and Dad actually agreed on something?" Julianna suspiciously questioned her and patted her new pet. "I love him very much."

"The puppy or your father?" her mother asked in a slightly amused tone. "Come sit with me, Julie. I need to tell you something very important."

"What's up, Mom?" Julianna asked, leaving the puppy to take a seat across from her mother at the maple kitchen table. "Is something wrong?"

"Before your father left for work today, he and I had a long talk," her mother stated in a sobering tone, between sips of tea.

"About the puppy?" Julianna asked, intently staring at her mother. "I'm going to call him Freckles."

"That's nice, Julie," her mom said, sounding somewhat distracted. "That's not all we talked about, dear. You see, your father and I have decided to separate."

Julianna stared at her mother with horrified eyes. "W-w-why?" she stammered, jumping up from her chair. "What happened?"

"Well, Julie, your father and I have very different priorities. Honestly, our love for each other has run dry," her mother replied. "Sadly, it's as simple as that."

"Simple?" Julianna exclaimed. "You call this simple? This is the worst day of my life!" Julianna screeched. "I lost my best friend and my family! I hate my life!" She stomped her way through the kitchen and down the hallway. Tears spilled from her blue eyes as she rushed up the stairs and into her bedroom.

After school, Courtney greeted her own mother as she walked into her industrial sized kitchen. "Hi, Susan," she said halfheartedly. "How's life?"

"Courtney! Hello," her mother said, looking up from the booklet she was reading to face her youngest daughter. "How was school?"

"It's never fun," Courtney shrugged and reached past her mother for the plate of freshly baked cookies that sat on the granite countertop.

"Well, I'm glad your day was good," her mother commented sarcastically. "Tonight, your father and I are attending a dinner party at the Taylors'. I left the number by the kitchen telephone. Don't stay up too late, okay?"

"Yeah, sure," Courtney shrugged. "I'm going over Alyssa Kelly's house tomorrow off the bus. Don't expect me home until Saturday."

"Just leave her phone number and address in your father's office," her mother replied, looking back down to the business proposal.

"Well, I would, but I don't have her number or her address," Courtney answered, between bites of cookie. "Sorry."

"Courtney, I understand that you might not have her number, but how do you expect me to reach you?" her mother asked, looking up from the proposal. "It is important that I would be able to if needed."

"You could buy me a cell phone," Courtney suggested.

"Seriously Courtney," her mother remarked, looking eye to eye with her youngest daughter. "I think it's time that you and I become more like mother and daughter than friends. From now on, I want to know whom you are with, where you are, what time you'll be home, and how I can reach you."

"Susan," Courtney began, as though she were talking to a little kid, "I'd rather have a friend than a mother. You're doing a good job; let's keep it that way. Okay?"

"Courtney," her mother said, shaking her head. "I don't know what to do with you."

"Nothing," Courtney said, flashing a sweet smile. "I'm perfect the way I am."

Mrs. Angeletti stared at her daughter through the sky blue eyes Courtney had inherited. Although they hadn't spent any quality time together since their June trip to the Hamptons, Mrs. Angeletti had noticed something was different about her daughter. Courtney had always dressed casually, worn little makeup, and valued the simple things in life. Suddenly Courtney seemed to have transformed into a little woman. Her hair now fell freely to her shoulders, escaping the bonds of her usual ponytail. Her chapstick had been replaced by frosted lip-gloss. In place of her backpack was a designer leather tote bag. Instead of being laced into sneakers, her feet were now raised on three-inch platform heels. Mrs. Angeletti could easily pinpoint Courtney's physical changes, but she felt uneasy about her daughter's recent attitude adjustment. She wanted to write it off as typical fourteen-year-old behavior, but the change in Courtney was continuing to concern her.

"You're right," Mrs. Angeletti agreed firmly. "Let's spend the rest of the day together. I can finish my work later tonight. How about we go to the mall, and I buy you that cell phone?"

Courtney shrugged. "Fine, as long as Dad pays the bill."

After school, Marielle entered her contemporary home and greeted her golden retriever. "Hi, Angel," she said. "How was your day?" Not expecting an answer from her loyal pet, Marielle strolled into her kitchen. While listening to the messages on her answering machine, she searched through the refrigerator for something to eat. The last message was from her mother, informing Marielle that she should start cooking dinner at four forty-five. *Thanks, Mom,* Marielle thought. *You know how much I love to cook.* The kitchen phone began to ring as Marielle decided to make a sundae. Grabbing a pint of ice cream from the freezer, she reached for the telephone. "Hello?" she said.

"Hi," a soft unsteady voice responded. "What's up?"

"Hey, Julie!" Marielle replied, recognizing her friend's voice. "Is something wrong?"

"Well, actually, very wrong," Julianna sobbed. "My parents are splitting up."

"Since when?" Marielle asked, selecting a large bowl from a dark cherry cabinet. "That is horrible!"

"Tell me about it!" Julianna exclaimed sadly. "It's the worst. They bought me a Dalmatian, as if it would make up for ruining my life."

"Oh, Julie," Marielle said sympathetically, "at least they got you a puppy. Just that shows they were thinking of you."

"Yeah," Julianna sobbed, "that's true. I knew you would see the positive side of this rather than the negative. That's why I didn't call Courtney. She hasn't been much of a friend lately."

Marielle and Julianna got into a long conversation about Courtney and divorce. Marielle's parents had separated a month after she was born, so she knew the pain of not having a father around. She hadn't seen her father since the divorce was final. When she tried to remember him, all she could envision was the man with dark brown hair on the cover of her parents' wedding album. Marielle reminded Julianna that she was lucky to even know her father and that the separation did not have to be permanent.

Angel suddenly began barking loudly, diverting Marielle's attention from Julianna. Marielle glanced at the clock on the kitchen wall. Four fifty-five. "Oh my gosh!" she exclaimed, hearing a car door slam shut. "Julie, I'm sorry but I have to go! I'll call you later if I can. Bye!"

Racing to hang up the telephone, Marielle searched through her kitchen cabinets. She selected a can of small shrimp, sliced potatoes, and diced tomatoes. After placing a pan filled with hot water on her electric cook top, Marielle retrieved a box of ziti from the lazy Susan. When her mom entered the kitchen, Marielle was confident that she appeared organized. "Hi, Mom," Marielle said, glancing up from the stove to her mother. "Supper should be ready soon."

"Really?" her mother questioned her, placing her brief case on the kitchen counter. "And how do you expect the water to boil if the stove is off?"

Marielle's eyes traveled to the cook top. Indeed, the knob read OFF. "I am such an idiot! How could I forget to turn the stove on?"

"Well, if you do things in a rush then you usually do not do them well," her mother remarked. "You will be a great cook some day, Marielle."

"Thanks," she replied, turning the knob to HI. "Oh my gosh, I wanted to tell you! Mr. and Mrs. Camen are splitting up!"

"Julianna's parents?" her mother asked, opening the can of shrimp. "When did you hear that?"

"Julianna called me after school. She was hysterical," Marielle explained, adding a teaspoon of oil to the water.

"Marielle, did you forget?" her mother asked, scooping the miniature shrimp into a bowl. "I'm sure it was very important for you to speak with Julianna, but you're grounded from the phone."

"I still don't understand why!" Marielle cried, adding a cup of ziti to the bubbling water.

"Why?" her mother exclaimed. "I gave you four hundred dollars to buy school clothes right?"

"Right."

"You bought more expensive clothes than I own!" her mother cried. "A black suede pea coat! You bought wool suits, khaki suits, cotton suits—all designer brands. Let's not mention the black, tan, white, and brown leather shoes! Um, what else —"

"Mom, I told you; I got good deals!" Marielle interrupted her. "Don't even accuse me of shop-lifting!"

"Marielle, I'm not stupid. Courtney, bought you that stuff with her parents' money," Mrs. Kayne said. "The money I gave you went as far as the dress pants and sweaters!"

"You know Courtney," Marielle whined, dramatically throwing her arms up in the air. "She bought everything I said I liked! When we got back to her house, she said, 'Oops! I must have grabbed the wrong sizes in all these clothes. Hey, they would fit you! Take them.'"

"Once again, Marielle, I'm not stupid!" Mrs. Kayne sighed. "You must have known what she was doing."

"I didn't!" Marielle exclaimed, stomping her heels on the ceramic floor.

"Control yourself!" Mrs. Kayne yelled. "Do you want to get grounded for another week? You could have cracked the floor with a temper like that!"

"I hate you," Marielle stated coldly, and then stomped through the house to her bedroom.

After school, at his home, Chris greeted his sister. "Hi, Katie," he said as she walked into the cluttered living room.

"You are such a loser," she stated without glancing in Chris' direction.

Chris sighed. "I can't believe a sixth grader is shooting me down," he muttered to himself, while turning back to his homework.

"What are you doing?" Katie asked, appearing beside him a moment later. Chris glanced over at her. She was peering at him with her hands on her hips. "Well?" she questioned him.

"I'm doing my homework," Chris responded and turned away from her.

Katie stared wide-eyed at her brother. "Are you sober?" she asked.

"Yes!" he exclaimed in an annoyed tone, although he knew her question was valid. "Yes, Katie, I am sober and trying to finish my Algebra homework."

"That's a first," she commented dryly. "What time are your friends coming over?"

Chris slammed his book shut. "They're not," he said, leaning back in his chair. "No more parties, Katie. I promise."

"Really?" she asked, softening her expression.

Chris nodded. "You were right; I've been pretty terrible to you," he admitted. "But I promise, that's all going to change. From now on I'm going to focus on school and football. I have my future to think about, and I've been heading down the wrong road long enough."

Bryan, who also went home after school, stumbled list-lessly into his house and rubbed his aching head. Without greeting his family, he climbed up the stairs and crawled to his bedroom. His phone was ringing when he entered the room. "Hello?" he moaned, picking up the receiver.

"Hi, Bryan!" a perky female voice responded. "What's up?"

"Who is this?" he asked, falling back onto his bed. "Courtney!" he exclaimed as he sat up straight in recognition of her voice.

"Of course," Courtney replied. "What's up?"

"Hey!" Bryan cried happily, suddenly not noticing his headache. "What's up with you?"

"Well, my mom just bought me a cell phone, and I wanted to test it out," Courtney explained. "My fingers absentmindedly dialed your number."

"I'm glad you called," Bryan admitted. Courtney fell completely silent. "Hello?" Bryan called, knowing how common it was for cell phones to drop calls. "Court?"

"Do you want me to call you?" Courtney questioned him hesitantly.

"Of course," Bryan laughed.

"Bryan, I better go," Courtney responded, hanging up quickly. The dial tone that rang into Bryan's ear stung both his headache and his heart.

six

"**A**lyssa!" Courtney called, walking over to her new friend on the second day of school. "What's up, girl?"

"Not much," Alyssa replied, walking beside Courtney down the cluttered corridor. "Did you bring your bus note?"

"Got it right here," Courtney replied, fetching the note from her pocketbook. "Oh, and check out my new phone," she added, holding up her shiny black phone.

"That's sick!" Alyssa exclaimed. "Hey! Cathy!" she yelled down the hallway.

"Hi!" Cathy replied, slamming her locker shut. "What's up?"

"Check out Court's new phone," Alyssa said when she reached Cathy's locker.

"Nice," Cathy replied, stealing the phone from Courtney's hand. "You know you could get in trouble for having this in school, right?"

"Then give it back to me and maybe no one will notice," Courtney responded matter-of-factly.

"Sorry," Cathy apologized and handed the phone back to Courtney. "Let's go to homeroom."

"Why?" Courtney questioned her. "We don't have to be there yet."

"She's right," Alyssa said.

"Bathroom," the three girls stated in unison.

"Did either of you guys see Chris?" Courtney asked on their way to the nearby ladies room.

"I did," Cathy answered. "He was walking with Jason; they seemed pretty tense. It was kind of weird to see. Jay's never serious, unless it has to do with school work, and they definitely were not discussing that."

"Really?" Courtney asked, pushing the bathroom door open. "I hope Jay's not mad at Chris for canceling his party."

"No way," Alyssa said, shaking her head as she followed Courtney through the bathroom door. "Jay might be a thorn in the side to most of us, but he doesn't get mad easily. They've been best friends for ten years. There's more to friendship than a stupid party."

Later on that day, Alyssa and Courtney waltzed through the double doors that led to the high school's courtyard. It was eighty degrees, sunny, and way too nice of a day to eat lunch inside. "Oh great," Alyssa sighed, reaching the table where their friends were gathered. "Who's in my seat?" she asked, peering at Jon expectantly.

"I am," Jon responded, warily eyeing his girlfriend. "That's because Cathy took mine."

"Only because Jason took mine!" Cathy exclaimed defensively. "You can sit there," she shrugged, pointing to the only available seat.

"What about Court?" Alyssa asked, taking a seat between Bryan and Jeff Brooke.

"You can sit here, Court," Bryan offered, rising from his seat. "I'll go sit with Chantal and Andy."

"No, that's okay," Courtney responded hesitantly, wondering how the seats had been labeled. After all, no one at the table had ever eaten in the courtyard. Was there some sort of social protocol she was unaware of? "We can just share the seat."

"Okay," Bryan agreed as his eyes lit up. "Fine with me."

"Court, let's go buy lunch," Alyssa suggested from the other side of Bryan.

"Okay," Courtney agreed, placing her hands on Bryan's shoulders. "Cathy, come with us."

"Thanks," Cathy replied, rolling her glassy green eyes. "I feel so privileged."

Alyssa glanced at Cathy with a perplexed expression.

"Hey, where's Chris?" Courtney asked, suddenly noticing his absence.

"He went to buy a drink," Jason informed her. "You should just take his seat—permanently." Courtney eyed Jason strangely, finding herself taken back by his comment.

As Courtney, Alyssa, and Cathy walked across the large courtyard, Courtney lost herself in thought. Why hadn't Chris saved her a seat? She had hardly spoken with him since yesterday's lunch, and even then, he had seemed distant. She thought back to Jon's Fourth of July party and the very moment she had spotted Chris staring at her through the fire. She remembered thinking he was cute—dressed nicely in a collared polo, khaki shorts, and a Red Sox hat. It wasn't until Jason came over and introduced Chris that she had felt any attraction towards him. When Bryan told her that Chris was the one everyone went to for *fun*, she had grown immediately interested in getting to know him. Chris had not even seemed surprised when she joined him by the water—as if they had telepathically planned their whole lives to sit there. She remembered how strange it had felt to feel so comfortable with someone whose voice she had never heard.

"Courtney!" a loud voice projected from the lunch line. "Courtney!"

"Did someone just say my name?" Courtney asked, escaping from her contemplation. "Oh, Chris," she sighed, spotting him near the front of the line.

"Hi," he greeted her when she rushed to his side. "What's up?"

"Nothing really," Courtney replied. "What's up with you?"

"Nothing," Chris said and smiled, affectionately placing his hand on Courtney's shoulder. "So, you're going over Alyssa's today?"

Courtney nodded.

"Yeah, that's what Cathy said."

"You're coming tonight, right?"

"I don't think so," he replied, reaching for a bottle of water. "I want to talk to you about that, okay? Go get your lunch and then we can walk around the school."

"Okay," Courtney agreed, finally understanding why Chris had not saved her a seat. "Wait for me when you get out of line."

Chris smiled and looked away from his girlfriend. How was he going to explain why he wasn't going to Jason's party without getting her mad? Chris did not expect her to understand because she had no idea what Jason's parties were like. Jason had two older brothers who were just as much trouble as he was. They were loud, usually intoxicated, jocks with plenty of alcoholic friends. Then again, the Courtney whom Chris had first met would have been able to take care of herself, even at a Davids' party. Chris was not so sure about this "new" Courtney.

Courtney selected a dark green tray and then quickly joined Alyssa and Cathy in line. "Hi," she greeted them. "Sorry it took me so long. Chris said he wants to talk to me."

"About him and Jay?" Alyssa asked, abruptly turning from Cathy to face Courtney.

"No," Courtney shook her head, "about his party."

"What about it?" Alyssa questioned her, progressing further ahead in line.

"I don't think he's going," Courtney replied with a confused expression on her face.

"Don't worry yourself too much," Alyssa comforted her. "I know Chris has been acting boring lately, but he'll show up. He'll probably be half-baked by the time he gets to Jay's, but at least he'll be himself."

"Maybe he's going to dump me!" Courtney exclaimed.

"I'm sure that's not it at all," Cathy spoke up, eyeing Courtney strangely. "What reason would he have to dump you?"

Courtney shrugged. "Do you think he found out about Bryan?"

"Found out *what* about Bryan?" Alyssa and Cathy questioned her in unison.

"No, that can't be it," Courtney said distractedly. She was the only one who knew she had called him.

"Maybe he has to stay home and baby-sit Katie," Cathy reasoned.

"Probably," Alyssa agreed. "If it will make you feel better, we can come with you for your talk with Chris."

"Would you?" Courtney asked, reaching for a bottle of water. "That would be great."

Cathy and Alyssa flashed wide smiles.

A few moments later, as they walked towards Chris, Courtney observed the worried look plastered across his face. "He's going to dump me," Courtney whispered tensely to Alyssa and Cathy.

"No, he's not! Just talk to him," Alyssa urged, pushing Courtney into Chris.

"I thought we were going to talk?" Chris questioned her, glancing from Courtney to the other girls.

"Whatever you say to me, they can hear," Courtney retorted. The butterflies in her stomach were killing her patience. "What's going on?"

"I wish we had some privacy," Chris said, eyeing Courtney intently.

"They're staying," Courtney stressed. "Why aren't you going to Jay's tonight?"

Chris sighed. "Look, Court, this is going to sound crazy, but I'm just sick of parties," Chris replied and turned away from her. "Maybe if it wasn't at Jason's house, then I would go."

"What's up with you guys?" Courtney asked, turning Chris around to face her.

"Nothing," Chris replied, glancing to the ground. "I just

don't want to go to another party. I'd rather you not go either."

Courtney dropped her jaw. "I can't believe you just said that!" she laughed. "You can't boss me around! I'm going to Jay's party tonight with Alyssa. That plan has already been made."

"Courtney—"

"I never would have gone out with you if I'd have known you'd be like this!" Courtney interrupted him.

"No, Court, listen to me," Chris pleaded. "I really don't want you to go to Jay's party. If you go, I can guarantee you will get in trouble. The Davids' parties are out of control."

Courtney lowered her eyebrows and glared at her boyfriend. She felt as if she were talking to Bryan. Bryan had always tried to keep her away from his friends. Bryan had always tried to protect her from getting into trouble. That was what she could not stand about him! She hated being sheltered and controlled. Bryan had always said, "My friends are no good," and expected her to just accept that. Courtney, however, wanted to use her own judgment and make her own decisions.

"Geez Chris, lay off of her," Alyssa spoke up from behind Courtney. "She'll be fine with us at Jay's tonight."

"Alyssa, just shut up!" Chris exclaimed and rolled his eyes. "You have no idea what you're talking about. Just stay out of this."

"That was real nice, Chris," Courtney rebuked, looking eye to eye with him. "Have a nice lunch," she added, quickly pushing past her stunned boyfriend.

seven

"I don't think so," Marielle spoke sadly into her telephone on Friday afternoon. "My mom almost grounded me for another week yesterday, and I'm not even supposed to be on the phone. Chantal, I can nearly guarantee the answer will be no."

"Are you sure? Can't you just ask?"

"Oh, no!" Marielle exclaimed. "Then she'll know I was on the phone after school. I really wish I could sleep over though."

"Just tell her that I asked you in school," Chantal suggested enthusiastically. "It's the truth."

"I'll try," Marielle agreed, clearing Chantal's number from the caller ID. "But don't expect me unless I call. My mom should be home any minute, so I better go."

"Hope to hear from you," Chantal chanted. "Bye."

"Bye," Marielle replied, placing the phone into its receiver. She still did not understand why she was grounded. Her mother was so unfair!

Marielle felt as if she hadn't spoken with Courtney in years. Since talking to Julianna was depressing, Marielle had decided that she needed a new friend—not a best friend, but a good friend. She and Chantal had clicked right away. There was something different about Chantal, something genuine. Somehow Marielle felt more comfortable with her than with her own best friends.

"I don't see why you didn't dump Chris," Alyssa stated as she and Courtney stepped off of her bus. "He was such a jerk to you today."

"To you too," Courtney agreed, observing the houses that lined Alyssa's development. They were all Victorian homes, but none were as large as the Angeletti's mansion.

"Yeah, well I'm kind of used to it by now," Alyssa said. "Chris and Jason aren't the nicest guys to hang out with. I still don't get why everyone makes such a big deal out of them."

"But, I mean, he is entitled to his own opinion," Courtney mumbled, looking down at her black leather sandals.

"Well, he obviously doesn't think that I'm entitled to my own!" Alyssa exclaimed.

"Guys are just hypocrites in general," Courtney replied, shrugging helplessly. She glanced up at Alyssa, surprised to see her lighting up a cigarette. Courtney knew that Chris and a lot of his friends smoked, but Alyssa seemed way too clean-cut for the habit.

"Here," Alyssa said and offered Courtney her cigarette. "You smoke, don't you?"

"Well...sometimes," Courtney lied, taking the cigarette from her friend. She hoped she did not look as intimidated as she felt. Why would Alyssa assume she smoked? She had never smoked anything in her life!

"I thought Chris said you did," Alyssa added, peering at

Courtney expectantly.

"I'm usually trying to get him to quit," Courtney replied, nervously holding the cigarette between her fingers. Did all of her new friends smoke? Would she have to pretend to smoke to meet their standards? Why would Chris lie? Was he embarrassed about her morals? He knew she hated drugs!

"Then someone's a hypocrite," Alyssa teased as Courtney hesitantly took a drag of the cigarette.

Courtney laughed as she exhaled, trying to hide how disgusted she was by the lingering taste in her mouth and her own weak behavior.

"Chris was the first one of our friends to smoke a cigarette; good luck trying to get him to quit," Alyssa laughed. "Jon and Jason have been giving him crap about it for the past three years. He doesn't care that his two best friends think it's disgusting."

"It's always worth a try. I almost got Bryan to quit when we were dating. He gave up everything else," Courtney said, hoping Alyssa would take back her cigarette. The last thing she wanted was for anyone to see her holding it. She was the mayor's fourteen-year-old daughter!

"I haven't seen Bryan smoke in a long time," Alyssa commented. "I'm pretty sure you got him to quit."

Courtney shrugged. "Maybe. I don't really see him much anymore. How long of a walk do we have to your house?" she asked, peering ahead at the line of large homes. She suddenly felt overwhelmed with anxiety.

Alyssa shrugged. "Another few minutes or so. My parents aren't home, so don't worry about smelling like smoke. Are you nervous about Jay's party tonight?"

Courtney shook her head and quickly handed the cigarette back to Alyssa. "I would be if I wasn't going with you. Jay is more of Chris' friend than mine, and I don't even think they're on speaking terms."

"Yeah, but everyone likes you," Alyssa stressed before taking a drag of her cigarette. "Knowing Jay, he invited you because he wants you," Alyssa added. "Seriously, he must have asked me five times today if you were coming!"

"Really?" Courtney asked. "He wants me even though he's with Cathy?"

"Jay just wants someone there to hit on when he gets in a fight with Cathy tonight," Alyssa clarified and tossed her cigarette to the ground. "Their relationship is terrible."

"Well, I know Bryan will be there, so that should make my night interesting," Courtney said quietly.

"Oh, Courtney, you still like him!" Alyssa sang with widening eyes. "Don't even try to deny it. Do you realize your face lights up when you hear his name?"

"Stop!" Courtney blushed.

"I knew it!" Alyssa exclaimed. "This is so perfect, Court! Bryan will be there, and Chris won't. Maybe you guys can talk and work things out. Maybe you'll both get drunk and then when—"

Perhaps it is best that Chris isn't going to the party, Courtney thought. *Bryan will be there, and maybe it will give me a chance to figure things out with him.* In the meantime, she needed to figure some things out for herself. What world was she stepping into? What was she welcoming into her life? Saying no to drugs had always been easy for Courtney. Why hadn't she been able to tell Alyssa that she didn't smoke? Was she seriously becoming that weak of a person? Why did she feel the need to be accepted to the point of rejecting her own morality?

Courtney thought back to Chris' party, remembering how out of control Chris and Jason had been. She had never seen intoxicated people act that way. Honestly, she suspected they had been on some sort of hallucinogenic. Asking Chris would have been pointless; she knew he couldn't remember anything from that night. Asking Jason was out of the question; he was the most intimidating kid Courtney knew.

Courtney had hoped to rub off on Chris, as she had on Bryan. Now, she began wondering if she were the one being influenced. Were Chris and his friends rubbing off on her? A small voice inside of her caught her attention. "Bad company corrupts good morals," it spoke. That was the voice Courtney had been drowning out for weeks, even though she knew it was the voice of Truth.

eight

That same evening, Chantal greeted Marielle at the front door of her home. "Hey! I was just about to go outside to wait for you. Here, let me help you with your stuff."

"Thanks," Marielle replied, handing Chantal her pillow. "Sorry if I'm early, but my mom figured she could drop me off on her way to the supermarket. I didn't want to argue with her, and I didn't want to go food shopping either. I'm just so glad she let me come! Sometimes I think she is two different people."

"It's fine," Chantal laughed and led Marielle up a set of stairs.

"Where's your sister?" Marielle asked, following Chantal to the top of the stairs.

"At a party," Chantal answered, turning down the hallway towards another flight of stairs. "My room and Cathy's room are up on the third floor, but my little sister's and my parents' rooms are down that hall," she explained and pointed down the long, second floor hallway.

"Your house is nice," Marielle remarked, proceeding up the stairs behind Chantal. "I think Courtney and your sister went to the same party. It was at Jason Davids', right?"

45

Chantal nodded. "Yeah, Cathy said something about Courtney getting ready with Alyssa. She sounded kind of jealous."

"A lot of people are jealous of Courtney," Marielle commented, entering Chantal's large bedroom. "I've been best friends with her since third grade, and sometimes, I'm even jealous of her."

"I don't think Cathy is jealous of Courtney; I think she's just jealous of the way Alyssa is treating her," Chantal stated thoughtfully as she placed Marielle's pillow onto her neatly made bed. "Cathy's territorial like that."

"See, Courtney's not like that," Marielle said, dropping her bag to Chantal's hardwood floor. "I'm beginning to doubt how much she really fits in with her new clique. She, Julianna, and I always hung out. Now, she purposely makes Julianna cry and hasn't called me all week. She's been different ever since she started hanging out with Chris. What do his parties do to people?"

"Well, I went to a couple parties at Chris' when I was going out with Jon," Chantal said, sitting down on her plush bedroom couch. "One of them was really bad. Mostly everyone went crazy rebellious, including my sister. She met Jason at that party and went downhill from there. Now she's practically an alcoholic and burnout."

"She changed that much in one night?" Marielle asked.

"Oh no! That party was during seventh grade," Chantal clarified.

"Oh okay," Marielle said, letting out a sigh of relief. "So what was the party like itself?" she pressed, hoping her curiosity would not annoy Chantal.

"I didn't stay long, but long enough to get in a fight with Jon," Chantal said and rolled her eyes. "Chris was passing around a blunt, and Jon took a few hits—not to mention he was already drunk. Jon had always claimed to be 'against drugs,' so seeing him do that made me really upset. I tried to tell him, but he wasn't interested in anything I had to say. After our fight, I felt uncomfortable, so Alyssa and I left the party."

"That was nice of her to leave with you," Marielle commented, glancing at the pictures lining Chantal's walls. The majority of them were of Chantal and her boyfriend, Andy Rosetti. There were a few of Jon and even some of Alyssa. "I'm sure she'll do the same for Courtney; they're becoming wicked close."

"Did you tell Courtney what I said about Alyssa?" Chantal asked, eyeing Marielle questioningly.

Marielle shook her head. "I decided to mind my own business."

"I felt really bad after I told you what happened to me. I shouldn't have said anything to taint your perspective of Jon or Alyssa," Chantal admitted nervously.

"No. I really appreciate you telling me about Courtney's new friends," Marielle assured her, sitting down on Chantal's queen-size bed. "I'm not exactly jealous of all the attention she's paying them, but I do miss her."

"Don't worry. She and Alyssa won't stay close for long," Chantal concluded sympathetically.

"Well, Courtney does seem happy," Marielle said, studying an old picture of Cathy and Chantal on Chantal's wicker nightstand. Marielle struggled to tell them apart because they both looked happy. If Cathy had once been as happy as Chantal, then why had she changed?

"In our middle school, all the girls wanted to be Courtney's friend, and all the guys wanted to date her. I always assumed it was because of her father," Marielle explained. "She never really felt the need to befriend everyone. She was happy just goofing around with Julianna and me. This summer when she started dating Chris, her priorities changed completely. She became consumed with her looks and popularity, instead of going to church or being a good friend. I'm getting kind of worried about her."

"Maybe someday I'll get to know her, but not if she's friends with Alyssa," Chantal shrugged. "Honestly, I have never resented anyone more than Alyssa in my entire life. It's awful. I should not hold resentment, and I know that. I just—I've never been so hurt in my life. Jon was my love, you know? I know I still love him. I'm pretty sure I always will. I feel so bad talking about them, but everything I say is true. I just don't want to see Courtney fall into the trap I did."

"What's Alyssa like?" Marielle asked.

"She's different now than she was when I knew her," Chantal said quickly. "I'm probably not the best person to ask because of the negative feelings I have towards her. She used to be awesome: fun, friendly, and loyal. I don't know what happened. Bad company corrupts good morals. That's for sure. She's gotten into most of the stuff the rest of her crew is into. The stuff they do is messed up."

"Courtney doesn't sound like them at all," Marielle stated, shaking her head.

"It's actually really sad because most of those kids are really nice people. In sobriety, Jason and Chris are awesome. Seriously, they're like the nicest guys I know. Bryan's a sweetheart too. I don't think Bryan's as bad as the rest of them. I honestly don't know anything about Jon anymore. I pray for him all the time. I don't understand how he can be comfortable living in darkness. He was raised as a Christian. I know he loves God. I never expected him to backslide. I can't even talk about it, or I will get upset. It's so sad."

"What girls do they hang out with besides Alyssa and Cathy?" Marielle pressed.

"Oh, Lisa Ankerman, Leslie Lucus, and Katherine Rossi," Chantal replied, pointing to their pictures on her wall. "Katherine's nice."

"Isn't your boyfriend friends with them?" Marielle asked as she recalled seeing all three of them at Andy's locker.

Chantal nodded. "Yeah. Lisa is Andy's childhood best friend. They're like brother and sister. Lisa dates Jeff Brooke, our class treasurer. Katherine dates Andy's best friend, Bobby Ryan, and Leslie dates Adam Case. Andy, Bobby, Adam, and Jeff have been tight for years. They're heavily involved with student council and sports. Bobby's a star football player like Chris. Andy, Jeff, and Adam all play hockey together."

"So their girlfriends hang out with Cathy instead of you? That's surprising," Marielle commented, lowering her eyebrows in confusion.

"They do a good job at looking perfect from the outside, but God gave me the discernment to stay away from them. I don't want anything to do with my sister's life-style. It leads to nowhere but destruction," Chantal explained. "When Jon and I broke up, I chose to shy away. It gets kind of lonely, but I pray daily for the strength not to compromise. Honestly, Andy and my mom are the only people I'm close with anymore. After being betrayed by your best friend and your boyfriend, it's hard to trust anyone. I miss my friends; I really do, but I can't surround myself with darkness. Light has no place with darkness, and God's given me the wisdom to flee from temptation. I know He hears my prayers and that He will bring friends into my life that will edify my walk. He has a plan and knowing that is enough for me."

"I hope Courtney stays as strong in her faith as you have," Marielle remarked, glancing at the pictures on Chantal's wall. "I'd hate to see her follow Jon's footsteps."

nine

Jason's house was nearly a two-mile walk from Alyssa's home. His house rested high on a hill, and Courtney's muscles ached as she trucked up his driveway. The cars that lined his driveway obviously did not belong to her fourteen-year-old friends. There were going to be a lot more people at Jason's party than the freshman class. They were people she would mean nothing to, and that intimidated her. Courtney's heart pounded hard against her chest as she and Alyssa climbed the cobblestone front steps.

An older teenager with a beer in his hand greeted the girls at the front door. "Jason, are these your friends?" he called, gesturing towards Courtney and Alyssa.

Jason entered the foyer and staggered towards the front door. "Ya Matt, let them in," he said, patting his brother on the shoulder. "What's up, guys?"

"You're obviously buzzing," Alyssa stated, walking past Jason into his elegant, two-story foyer.

"Hey, Court!" Jason greeted her, thrusting his arm around her and pulling her inside his home.

Courtney pulled away from his embrace. "Did Chris show up?" she asked eagerly.

"No, he made it clear that he wouldn't be," Jason replied, dragging her into the kitchen where their friends were huddled.

"Hi, guys!" Courtney exclaimed, brightly eyeing her friends. Jon, Cathy, Lisa Ankerman, Jeff Brooke, and Leslie Lucus surrounded a granite-topped counter.

"Hey, Court!" Jon cried in a very friendly tone. "Where's your man?"

Courtney shrugged. "I guess he's not coming out tonight. Is Bryan here?" she questioned him, hoping no one took her response out of context.

"Well, you see Court-ney," Jason sang, once again placing his arm around her shoulders, "I had some herb and a pipe. Jon, Bryguy, and a few others came over after school, so we pregamed up in my room. Some of my guests have brought me more weed, but my pipe and papers are upstairs."

"So Bryan went up to get them?" Courtney assumed, observing the puffiness beneath Jason's glassy eyes. She turned and studied Jon, who showed no sign of being high or drunk. She remembered Chris saying that Jon was straightedge, so she found Jason's words hard to believe. Jon seemed like a really good kid. He certainly stood out from the others.

The idea of Bryan smoking pot completely turned Courtney's stomach. She really expected him to be above that. Were Jason's words purposely misleading or was Courtney just naïve?

"Do you want something to drink?" Jason offered, tapping Courtney's shoulder.

"Ugh, not right now," Courtney replied, edging away from Jason. "Not ever," she added beneath her breath.

Flee the evil desires of youth, and pursue righteousness, faith, love, and peace, along with those who call on the Lord out of a pure heart, a small voice inside of her spoke. Courtney's eyes began filling up with tears as she became overwhelmed with conviction. What was she doing at a drug-infested party?

"Seeing that Chris isn't coming, I'm surprised you came," Cathy stated, eyeing Courtney coldly.

"Why?" Courtney questioned Cathy, walking towards her as she fought off tears. The coldness in Cathy's eyes added to Courtney's discomfort. It wasn't Courtney's fault that Jason kept hanging all over her!

"Hey!" Bryan exclaimed as he and Courtney collided. "Court, what's up?"

On instinct Courtney embraced him.

"What was that for?" Bryan asked, handing the pipe and papers to Jason. Courtney looked into Bryan's perfectly matte eyes. She was not going to risk getting into a serious conversation with someone under the influence. Despite what Jason had said, Bryan looked perfectly sober.

"Who wants a hit?" Jason sang as he began rolling a joint with the papers Bryan had handed him.

"You know I'm all set with that crap," Bryan responded, grabbing Courtney's hand and pulling her closer into his arms.

Cathy pushed past Courtney, in a less than friendly manner, as she made way to Jason. Courtney did not give Cathy the satisfaction of a glare in her direction. "What is stuck up her butt?" she whispered to Bryan.

Bryan shrugged and smiled. "Did Jay offer you a drink?" he asked, reaching into the nearly empty thirty-rack on the counter.

"Yeah, he did," Courtney replied, "but please don't drink tonight, Bry." She placed her left hand onto Bryan's arm and looked pleadingly into his eyes.

"All right," Bryan agreed easily. "What's going on?"

Courtney sighed and placed her head on Bryan's shoulder.

"Court, what's wrong?" Bryan asked, lifting up her chin and searching her eyes.

I miss you, Courtney thought. *That's what's wrong! I had you and then I let you go. Therefore, I am overcome with self-pity. I hate how I am acting. I just want to leave this party and run back to my comfort zone.* All she said was, "I don't know."

"What?" Bryan pressed, gently brushing a piece of jet-black hair from her flushed face.

"Do you think we could go somewhere and talk?" Courtney asked, raising a single eyebrow.

"Absolutely," Bryan said with a nod. "Hey, Jay?"

"Hey, what's up?" Jason replied, without glancing in Bryan's direction.

Bryan walked over to Jason with Courtney close behind him. "Can, uh, we go talk in your room?" he whispered.

Jason laughed loudly and glanced from Bryan to Courtney. "Ya dude, help yourself! There are some condoms in the nightstand if you need one!" Courtney dropped her jaw and widened her eyes in horror.

"Oh, shut up," Bryan demanded, pushing Jason hard in the shoulder. Obnoxious giggles escaped from their friends, and numerous pairs of eyes darted from Courtney to Bryan.

"Yay!" Alyssa clapped, sending a mischievous smirk in Courtney's direction. Courtney blushed deeply and followed Bryan out of the kitchen with her head down. The privacy she and Bryan had requested was for nothing other than a serious heart to heart. Jason had made it unrealistically clear otherwise.

"They are so obnoxious," Courtney complained, tightly gripping the cherry railing as she eased her way up the stairs.

"They're just playing," Bryan responded, reaching the grand second floor hallway. "They all like you a lot."

Courtney nodded without smiling. "I heard," she replied flatly. "So where's Jason's room?"

"Down this hall," Bryan led.

"I can't wait to breathe a breath of fresh air," Courtney sighed, halting behind Bryan at Jason's door.

"You won't find it in here," Bryan said, opening the door to a strong odor.

"This kid is absolutely ridiculous!" Courtney cried, shaking her head in disgust as she entered Jason's room. "Look around this room! He is seriously way too into drug paraphernalia. Don't his parents suspect anything? His walls are practically papered with pot leaf posters!"

"I don't know," Bryan shrugged carelessly.

"Chris' room isn't even this bad," Courtney added, wide-eyed.

"Court, do you want to talk somewhere else?" Bryan inquired.

"How much weed does this kid smoke?" Courtney rambled in amazement. "There is no way that he alone could have smoked all that today," she said pointing to a nearby ashtray with a few roaches in it. Bryan sighed and climbed over the remains of Jason's pre-party. "By the way," she sang nonchalantly.

"No," Bryan interrupted her, turning her petite body around to face him.

"No, what?" Courtney asked.

"Oh don't even give me that!" Bryan exclaimed with a

flirtatious smile.

He knows me too well, she thought. "Well, I want to know... when was the last time you smoked?"

"Smoked what?"

"Anything!" Courtney demanded loudly.

"Court, you know I quit smoking weed when I was with you," Bryan replied. "I may smoke a cigarette every once in a while, but not often. Why do you ask? Is it because I brought Jay down his pipe?"

"Forget it," Courtney responded, regretting any tension she had caused. She knew that Bryan would never lie to her. Bryan had never liked drugs to begin with. He had told her he only tried them because that was all his friends did for fun. She thought he had been joking when he said that was all they did. Now she understood exactly what he had meant.

"So what's up for real, Court?" Bryan asked, sitting down on Jason's unmade bed. He pulled her down beside him as pain filled her eyes.

"Oh Bry, I don't want to ruin the party for you," Courtney sighed. "You should be downstairs getting trashed with all your buddies."

"Not when someone I care about is upset," Bryan answered without hesitation.

Courtney smiled. Tears once again filled up her eyes. "How much is that?"

Bryan moaned. "Why are you doing this? Why are you avoiding what you really want to talk about?"

"I'm not," Courtney said, shaking her head and leaning closer to Bryan. "I want to talk about us."

ten

Chris Dunkin —9:00 p.m.

Why am I sitting at home, on my living room sofa, with my little sister on a Friday night? My best friend is having a party. My girlfriend is there. Why the heck am I watching Nick at Nite reruns? Is this the social level I have sunk to? I, "the life of the party" only two nights ago, am now a friendless, straightedge, low-life. What the heck!

Why is the girl who inspired me to make something of myself now acting so stupidly?

I'm sitting here without her, miserably fighting the undying urge to crack open a beer or smoke a bowl. But why have I let drugs become such a large part of my life? My friends were stupid to follow my path. What scares me the most is that I know even Jason is a follower of my path. Jason, the kid with the worst reputation in Montgomery, is a follower of mine! Jason's reputation was given to the wrong person—thank God. I was just "the life of the party" and glad at that.

I am pathetic, but I will say, less pathetic than I was two nights ago. I am a mess, a nervous wreck, and I'm having Courtney withdrawals: her pale blue eyes, her scent, the warmth that lines my body when I hug

57

her...but honestly, none of that is important to me if she's going to start acting like my friends. I'm looking for so much more than that.

Both today and yesterday, I couldn't tear my eyes off of this one brunette in my science class. Before this year, I never saw her or heard a thing about her. Her appearance is not exotically striking, but she is really cute. Her face continues to break through my thoughts of Courtney and that troubles me. Honestly, I'm finding myself less and less attracted to Courtney... but I do still care about her.

What am I going to do about her?

She's at a party with a bunch of wasted guys who are probably trying to take advantage of her, and I'm sitting here watching I Love Lucy. And I'm okay with that? No, definitely not.

Later on that evening, Marielle glanced up from the photo album she was perusing and said, "Tal, I think your phone is ringing."

"My gosh, I love this picture!" Chantal laughed, peeling her eyes away from a seventh grade snapshot of Jon, Chris, and Jason. "Hello?" she sang into her cordless phone.

"Hey, Chantal," a deep voice replied; "it's Chris."

Chantal's jaw dropped. "That's so weird! I was just looking at a picture of you."

"Really?" Chris asked her. "Well, uh, why?"

"Just for laughs," Chantal stated. "My friend Marielle is sleeping over, and she wanted to see it."

Chris laughed. "You should hang out with that girl more often."

"So, what's up?" Chantal asked, flipping to another page in her photo album. She pointed to a more recent picture of Chris. Marielle's eyes widened.

"Have you heard from Cathy at all?" Chris questioned her.

"No."

"Have you heard from anyone at the party?"

"You're there, aren't you?"

"No," he answered downheartedly. "But Courtney's there."

"Oh my gosh, Chris, what happened?" Chantal asked with concern. In spite of the fact that Chantal hadn't talked on the phone with Chris in over a year, she was not finding the conversation awkward at all.

Chris sighed. "We fought over Jason's party. I didn't want us to go, but she went anyway."

"Wait a minute," Chantal interrupted. "You didn't want to go?"

"Honestly, Tal, I didn't."

"That's really good," Chantal commended, recalling how deeply worried she'd been about her old friend. She had prayed for him multiple times that year.

"I'm worried about Courtney though," Chris confessed. "She is so innocent and naïve. The cops always show up at Jay's parties, and I know she's going to get in trouble. She didn't give me her cell phone number, Jay's phone is off the hook, and I have no way of getting in touch with her. Have you or your friend Marie heard from her?"

"Her name's Marielle," Chantal retorted, "and I don't know Courtney personally. I used to see her at church, but

I never talked to her. She hasn't been there in awhile."

"Oh."

"But Marielle has been best friends with her for years," Chantal added. "I'm sure Courtney's told you all about her."

"Seriously?" Chris asked, sounding bewildered. "Can you put her on the phone?"

Back at the party, Bryan stared intently at Courtney. "What?!"

"I'm going to break up with Chris," Courtney repeated. "I dumped you for him, and I regret it."

Bryan's heart began racing in his chest. "Wh-wh-why?" he stammered, shaking his head. "I don't understand."

"Bryan, I don't like him the way I like you," Courtney whined, running a hand through Bryan's hair. "You and I never fought once while we were together."

"True, but the breakup was pretty harsh, Court," Bryan commented.

"Yeah, I realize that; I'm sorry," Courtney replied, biting her bottom lip. "If I were to break up with Chris, would you take me back?"

"Courtney, what are you about?" Bryan questioned her and rose from Jason's bed.

"I'm not about anything," Courtney replied, standing up beside him. "I just want to apologize for hurting you so badly." She placed her hand over Bryan's pounding heart.

"Your apology is accepted," Bryan responded flatly and stared blankly ahead. He could not understand himself. He had been dreaming of a moment like this since their breakup. Why was he making it so difficult for her?

"Bryan, look at me," Courtney pleaded, turning him around to face her. "You still have it in you, don't you? I mean, you said a half-hour ago that you care for me. What were you getting at?"

Bryan sighed. "Court, I just don't know about you," he retorted, silently regretting his word choice. "I liked you so much, and you broke my heart because you decided I wasn't fun enough for you. Now you're about to break Chris' heart for whatever reason. Do you care about other people's feelings at all? I don't think I could put up with that kind of hurt again."

"Bryan, Chris and I got in a fight!" Courtney cried, placing her hands on her hips. "He's depressed or something and not acting like himself. I mean, since when did Chris not want to socialize?"

"Courtney, he's changing his ways for you," Bryan replied. "Just like I did."

"But he's not talking to me about it!" Courtney exclaimed with tears glazing her eyes. "I don't want to hurt him, but I can no longer deny the feelings that I still have for you."

"Chris and I are on poor terms as it is," Bryan commented, turning away from Courtney.

"Then you know what, Bryan? Forget it!" Courtney raged, stomping out of Jason's bedroom.

"Court?" Bryan called, chasing after her. Since their breakup, he'd wanted nothing more than Courtney back in his arms. *Oh no, oh no, oh no.* Had he blown it? "Courtney, wait!" Courtney halted at the top of the stairs with tears streaming down her face. Standing with her arms crossed, she kept her eyes locked on the floor. "Court," Bryan whispered upon reaching her, "I'm sorry." Before she could turn away from him, he lifted her chin. Looking eye to eye with her, he began wiping away her tears. "I want our relationship back so badly. Please, let's go back to Jay's room and talk."

Courtney turned away from him.

"I'm sorry, Court," Bryan stressed, taking her hand. "Please let's talk. Please?"

Courtney looked up and stared into Bryan's eyes. "Okay," she agreed softly and allowed him to lead her back to Jason's room.

At Chantal's house, Marielle continued her conversation with Chris. "So you want me to call her?" she inquired, referring to Courtney.

"I would love you if you called her," Chris replied. "Pleeease," he begged.

"She'll probably get mad at me," Marielle stated flatly. "Couldn't you just call her? I mean, she's already mad at you."

"That was terrible!" Chris exclaimed playfully.

"Well, I want to help you, and I don't want Court getting in trouble; it's just that I don't want to get on worse terms with her," Marielle explained.

Chris sighed.

"Listen, if you really want me to call her, I will," Marielle agreed, less than enthusiastically.

"Seriously?" Chris asked with his tone lightening.

"Yeah," Marielle said. "You seem like you really care

about her, and she deserves to know you're worried."

"Thanks, Marielle," Chris replied. "You seem like a really good friend. It's weird that I don't know you. Honestly, I don't even remember Courtney mentioning you. Then again, I don't have the clearest memory. Do you know who I am?"

"Chantal and Courtney have both shown me pictures of you," Marielle said, gazing at a collage on Chantal's wall. "And you're in one of my classes."

eleven

"Do you really mean that?" Courtney asked, staring intently at Bryan as they continued their conversation in Jason's bedroom.

Bryan nodded, embracing her in his arms. "Courtney, I want you back so badly. I'm sorry if I was a jerk a few minutes ago."

"It's okay, Bryan. I'm just so glad that you'd take me back," Courtney replied, hugging him tightly.

"I don't know how you're going to handle this with Chris, but I'm behind you all the way," Bryan pledged. "I know Chris and I aren't on the best of terms, but I don't really care. Having our relationship back is more important to me than anything."

"I'm so glad you feel that way, Bry. I do feel bad for Chris though," Courtney admitted. "The thing is, I don't want to hurt Chris in the least bit. He's been nothing but nice to me. I was the one at fault in our fight. I should have listened to what he had to say and probably shouldn't have come here. I knew you would be here, so I really wanted to come. When I called you yesterday, I realized I liked you more than I could ever like Chris. I know I can't lead on Chris. I told you before that I was drawn to him,

64

but I think I took it the wrong way. Maybe we were just meant to be good friends. Maybe he needed some positive reinforcement in his life."

"Just don't be harsh on him like you were on me, okay?" Bryan suggested.

"Maybe he's mad at me for coming here and wants me to break up with him," Courtney contemplated. "It's just a thought, but maybe he will break up with me!"

"Courtney, wouldn't that ruin your 'never been dumped' reputation?" Bryan teased.

Courtney shrugged. "I wouldn't care as long as I could go back out with you."

Bryan blushed. "I promise, as soon as you and Chris break up, I'll ask you back out."

"Really?" Courtney questioned him, raising both of her eyebrows.

Bryan nodded.

"And this isn't just some scheme you've planned to get back at me for hurting you?" Courtney asked, eyeing Bryan nervously.

"Court, you know I would never do that," Bryan responded, taking her left hand into his own. "I love you."

Meanwhile at Chantal's, Marielle hung up the telephone. "I can't get through," she said. "I hope everything is okay at the party."

"Everything's fine, Marielle. The music's probably so loud that she couldn't hear her phone ringing," Chantal stated.

"That's a thought," Marielle agreed. "Sorry that I've spent most of the night on the phone."

"It's all right," Chantal said with a smile. "You're doing Chris a favor, and I think that's really nice."

"What's Chris like?" Marielle asked, once again studying his picture.

"He's wicked cute, isn't he?" Chantal commented, following Marielle's eyes to Chris' picture.

Marielle nodded. "Yeah, Courtney's lucky."

"Chris is a really nice kid," Chantal began. "I'm sure you wouldn't guess from just looking at him, but he's a very compassionate person. He and I used to be close when I was going out with Jon. He's seriously someone you can't help but love. He can take anything and make it funny. I really miss hanging out with him.

"His parents go away a lot and leave him to look after his sister. Sometimes, they have his older cousins stay with them, but that's how Chris got messed up in the first place. In the past year or so, he's gotten pretty deep into drugs—stuff beyond weed and alcohol. He sounded different on the phone tonight. You know, kind of like he used to before—well—you know. Seriously, Courtney is lucky to be with him. He has a huge heart. I really hope he stays on the track she's got him on."

"What track is that?" Marielle asked.

"He just sounds like he has his head on straight again," Chantal replied. "Maybe Courtney's shined some light into his dark life."

Upstairs at the party, Courtney sighed as she rose from Jason's bed. "We should probably head back downstairs," she said.

"Yeah," Bryan agreed and followed Courtney, "before

anyone misses us."

Courtney yawned. "I almost forgot there was a party going on downstairs. I can only imagine who else has shown up."

"Hopefully not any cops," Bryan said as he opened Jason's poster-lined door.

"Yeah, that would really ruin things," Courtney agreed, walking down the deserted hallway. Bryan took Courtney's hand and led her down the stairs. Courtney withdrew her hand from Bryan's as they entered the kitchen where their friends had remained.

"Hey!" Jon greeted them, still appearing sober.

"Hey," Courtney and Bryan responded in unison.

"What have you two been up to?" Jason sang and patted Bryan's back.

"Oh leave them alone," Jon interrupted, walking over to Bryan and Courtney.

"What's up, buddy?" Bryan asked.

"This party really sucks when you're the only one sober," Jon replied.

"Are they drunk or baked?" Courtney asked, glancing over Jon's shoulder at Alyssa, Cathy, and the rest of the group.

Jon shrugged. "Does it matter? Alyssa is driving me crazy. Honestly, I don't even want to be here anymore. She was hanging all over me, so I was cool with that. Then she started drinking a beer, even though she knows I hate it when she drinks. The next thing I know, she's taking a haul of someone's cigarette, and that's not okay. I don't date girls who smoke, and I didn't think my girlfriend smoked! We've been together for over a year, and she's never smoked anything in front of me. So after I avoided her for a half-hour, she decided to take a hit off a joint Jay passed around."

"Really? I saw her smoke a cigarette after school today. You didn't know she smokes?" Courtney asked.

At the sound of Courtney's words, Jon's face turned red with anger. "No," he said flatly.

"What's gotten into her?" Courtney asked, peering at Alyssa. She was laughing hysterically and twirling Leslie Lucus around like a ballerina.

"I'm done with her; that's for sure," Jon stated sternly.

"Are you going to break it off?" Bryan asked, glancing from Jon to Alyssa.

"If she keeps this up? Yeah." Jon nodded intently. "Absolutely."

"Jay, I think your phone is ringing," Lisa Ankerman called from beside Cathy.

"It's not mine. Mine's off the hook," Jason replied. "Who has a cell phone?"

"Me!" Courtney squeaked, rushing towards her bag on the counter. "Oh my gosh! I forgot all about my phone! Crap, what if someone was trying to reach me? Hello?" she cried into the phone, blocking her other ear as she rushed out of the kitchen.

"Court?" Marielle inquired.

"Ugh, I can't hear you; wait a minute!" Courtney sighed and walked up Jason's stairs with Bryan and Jon. "Marielle?"

"Yeah, are you all right?" she asked.

"Kind of," Courtney answered. "Why, what's going on?"

"I'm at Chantal Kagelli's," Marielle replied, "and Chris called. He sounded kind of worried about you, so I said I'd give you a call. Where have you been? I've been calling since nine-thirty!"

"I didn't hear my phone," Courtney replied. "Bryan and I were upstairs talking, and I left my bag in the kitchen.

So, what's up?"

"Chris just wanted to know if you were okay," Marielle said. "You are, right?"

"Was he going to come get me?" Courtney asked, entering Jason's bedroom.

"He said something about his cousin who has a car," Marielle informed her. "He seemed really worried about you."

Wow—I can't believe he still cares... even after I was so rude to him. "Hold on, Mar," Courtney said, turning towards Bryan and Jon. "Do you guys want to get out of here?"

"Whatever," Bryan shrugged. Jon nodded intently and widened his already large brown eyes.

"Marielle, do you think Chris would still come get me?"

"Probably."

"And Jon and Bryan?" Courtney added, biting her bottom lip.

"I can call him and ask, if you want," Marielle offered willingly.

"Okay—call me back," Courtney requested, giving Jon and Bryan a thumbs up sign.

Marielle hung up with Courtney and turned towards Chantal. "She wants me to call Chris and ask him to go get her, Bryan, and Jon."

"Jon, too, huh? Figures he would be at the party. Well, then call Chris!" Chantal exclaimed, throwing her phone book at Marielle.

"I can't call him!" Marielle cried. "He'll think I'm weird

or something. He probably doesn't even remember who I am. You call him!"

"His brain is not that fried," Chantal laughed. "He's expecting your call. What is wrong with you?"

"Can you please call him?" Marielle asked. "Please, Chantal?"

Chantal rolled her eyes. "My gosh, you're acting like you like him or something." Marielle turned her back to Chantal. "Oh my gosh, you do!" Chantal said accusingly. "Look at me."

Marielle turned and faced Chantal with a hesitant smile veneering her lips. "I don't even know him."

"Then call him," Chantal smirked, gesturing towards the telephone. "You shouldn't be scared."

"I'm phone shy," Marielle said, regretting her lame response.

"Yeah, okay."

Marielle sent a playful glare in Chantal's direction and then continued to search for Chris' number. "Is there any certain order these numbers are in?"

Chantal shrugged. "Chris is somewhere in the beginning. My phonebook's in chronological order."

"Zero-six-three-five," Marielle read off, picking up the telephone. She didn't hesitate dialing his number; after all, he was expecting her call.

twelve

C hris sat by the kitchen telephone, shredding a piece of paper with his restless hands. "What the heck!" he shouted, stomping his bare feet on the ceramic-tile floor.

"Are you okay, Chris?" Katie called to him from the living room.

"Yeah, sorry," Chris replied, resting his chin in his hands and rubbing his forehead. Chris had the unshakable feeling that Marielle was the girl in his science class whom he had found attractive. While on the phone with her, he had been intrigued by her comments. She seemed laid back, agreeable, and considerate. She agreed to help him out at the risk of upsetting Courtney. Would Courtney do Chris an inconveniencing favor? By going to Jason's party she had answered that question.

The ringing telephone awoke Chris from his contemplation. "Hello?" he called, answering the cordless phone and walking outside onto his back porch. He took a seat on a lounge chair and pulled a cigarette out of his pocket.

"Hi, Chris?" Marielle's voice replied.

"Yeah, it's me," Chris replied after lighting his second cigarette of the day. He was trying his best to quit smoking, but he had become somewhat dependent on the vice. He had first tried smoking at age ten, and by age twelve, he had begun smoking habitually. After almost three years of smoking, how could he not expect to be addicted? Even though his group of friends considered smoking "socially acceptable," Chris had decided it did not suit the life-style he desired to live. In order to succeed in his football career, he would need all the lung capacity he could get. His cousin Marc, who was co-captain of MLH's varsity football team, had been pointing that out to Chris for years. Jon and Jason had repeatedly expressed similar concerns. Smoking was just another item on the long list of things Chris wished he had never tried.

"It's me—Marielle. I talked to Courtney, and she, um, wants you to pick up her and, um, Bryan and Jon," Marielle informed him.

"Are you serious? Bryan and Jon?" Chris complained.

"That's what she said," Marielle sang. "Do you still want to get her?"

"Yeah, it will just be kind of awkward," Chris said slowly as an idea entered his mind.

"Why?" Marielle asked. "Bryan and Jon are your friends, aren't they?"

Chris sighed. "Yeah, but it's screwed up."

"Oh," Marielle answered quietly.

"Hey!" Chris exclaimed brightly. "Would you and Tal want to come for a ride?"

"To get Courtney?" Marielle questioned him with a twist of surprise in her tone.

"Yeah, would you?"

"Hold on," Marielle replied. Chris' heart pounded as he waited for Marielle to discuss the situation with Chantal. He flicked his not-even-half-smoked-cigarette over the railing and walked back into his house. Saving Courtney from getting in trouble suddenly seemed less important as Marielle began to dominate his mind. Now that he knew Courtney was safe, he wanted to find out if Marielle was the cute girl from his science class.

"Chris?" Chantal's voice rang into his ear.

"Hey, Tal," Chris greeted her.

"What's going on?" she asked. "You want us to come with you to Jay's?"

"Could you please?" Chris pleaded.

"It's not too late, so my mom may let us come," Chantal replied. "Talk to Marielle while I go ask, okay?"

"Sure," Chris agreed with ease.

"Hey," Marielle spoke into the phone a second later.

"Hi," Chris said—a smile spread across his lips at the sound of her voice. "So I guess you might be coming with me, huh?"

"Yeah, if you want me to," Marielle replied. "I'm sure I could wait at Chantal's if the car will be too crowded."

"Don't be ridiculous!" Chris exclaimed. "I want you to come. I want to meet the person who's helped me so much tonight."

"That's cool," Marielle stated flatly. "So you really like Courtney, huh?"

"That came out of nowhere," Chris responded, pondering his answer.

"Sorry," Marielle retorted, "you just seem like you really care about her."

"Don't be sorry; I see where you're coming from," Chris stressed, hoping he hadn't made Marielle feel uncomfortable.

"I'm happy for Courtney," Marielle said, sounding at

ease. "She's lucky to have such a caring boyfriend. Whether she shows it or not, I'm sure she appreciates you." Chris sighed, wondering if he should tell Marielle how he *really* felt about Courtney. Chris was afraid she'd think he was weird if she knew the truth. Seriously, why would he go through so much trouble if he didn't love Courtney? He knew he must love her in some way. She had been such an inspiration to him. How could he not be there for her?

"Chris?" Marielle called. "Hello?"

"Oh sorry, Marielle," Chris apologized. "My, uh, little sister was calling me."

"That's okay," Marielle said. "Chantal says it's okay for us to go with you. Maybe you should check and see if your cousin can bring us."

"Yeah, okay," Chris said. "I'll call you back, okay?"

"Me or Chantal?"

"You."

At the party, Jon sat in the hallway outside of Jason's bedroom, deep in thought. He couldn't motivate himself to charge downstairs and break up with Alyssa. It wasn't that he loved her; it was more his own fear of another foolish breakup.

When Chantal had been Jon's girlfriend, he couldn't get enough of her. She was his dream girl: kind, loving, honest, loyal, and friendly, with a heart after God. The last message Chantal had left him said simply, "Jon, I can't deal with you or your games anymore. It's over. I'm through. You should just go out with Alyssa. She's the only one who has true feelings for you." It was cold and aloof, something he had never expected from Chantal.

How had his thoughts swayed towards Chantal? Alyssa was his girlfriend and current problem. She was downstairs—drunk and high—acting like an idiot. But that wasn't the Alyssa Jon knew! Had he done something to upset her? Was she purposely trying to upset him? Why had the last two years of Jon's life been filled with so much confusion and drama?

Jason's bedroom door creaked open, as Bryan and Courtney stepped into the hallway. Courtney pulled her hand from Bryan's grip when she noticed Jon. Refusing to meet Jon's eyes, she proceeded down the hallway towards the stairs. "Did you break up with her?" Bryan asked, staring anxiously at Jon.

Jon sighed and adjusted his baseball hat. "No," he said, glancing over the railing to the foyer below. "What's going on with you and Courtney?"

Bryan shrugged and looked down at the carpet.

"Did Marielle call back?" Jon questioned him, gripping the railing tightly as he trudged down the stairs.

"No," Bryan replied. "Dude, are you okay?"

Jon remained silent as he walked across the foyer. "Alyssa!" he shouted, angrily stomping through the kitchen doors. "What the heck is your problem?" The chant of the party fell silent. Heads turned, and eyes peered.

Alyssa turned to Jon as her glassy eyes filled with fear. "Jon?"

"Yeah, it's your boyfriend, letting you know you're an embarrassment!" Jon screamed. Alyssa stared at him blankly. "I've had it!" Jon continued, drawing more attention their way.

"Jon, what is wrong with you?" Alyssa asked quietly as her eyes began filling with tears.

"We're through," Jon stated flatly, looking eye to eye with her. "You've changed into someone I could never have a steady relationship with. I feel like I don't even know who you are. To this day, Chantal means more to me than you ever could. Go chew on that for awhile."

thirteen

A hot flash shot through Marielle's veins as Chantal's telephone began ringing. "Marielle, it's for you," Chantal sang, tossing her the cordless phone.

Marielle's hand shook as she placed the phone to her ear. "Hello?" she said as her heart skipped a beat.

"Hey, it's me," Chris responded coolly. "What's up?"

"Nothing's down," Marielle replied, attempting to calm her nerves.

"Well, that's good," Chris sang. "So what are you and Chantal up to?"

"Nothing really," Marielle said. "We were going to watch a movie, but there's really no point if we'll be going out."

"Oh yeah, what movie?"

"*Sydney White*," Marielle answered.

"Was that your pick or Tal's?"

"Both of ours."

"Can't you guys just watch it when you get back to Chantal's?"

"I guess."

"Maybe you could bring it with you, and we could watch it at my house," Chris suggested.

"What are you getting at?" Marielle accused playfully.

77

"Just that I'd like your company," Chris replied noncha-lantly.

Marielle froze. Was he flirting with her? "So you like that movie?" she asked, trying to figure him out.

"And you," Chris answered flatly.

"What?!" Marielle questioned him, suddenly feeling weak all over.

Chris laughed. "Don't sound so surprised. You seem like a pretty cool girl, and I like hanging out with cool people."

"O-kay," Marielle replied hesitantly, making eye contact with Chantal.

"What's he saying?" Chantal whispered.

"So you want to watch the movie with us?" Marielle questioned him.

"Yeah," Chris replied immediately.

"With Courtney, Bryan, and Jon too?" Marielle asked in confusion.

"If they want," Chris stated as though the idea had nev-er entered his mind.

"Can I ask you a question?" Marielle queried, glancing once again at Chris' school picture.

"Yeah, go ahead," Chris replied nonchalantly.

"Well, do you—like still, um, I don't know," Marielle stammered.

"What?" Chris asked. "You can ask me anything; I'm an open book."

"Well, are you and Courtney apart or something?" Ma-rielle blurted, hoping Chris was expecting that question.

"We're in a fight," Chris responded vaguely, "but I don't think we'll need to make up."

"What do you mean?" Marielle asked, wondering which way to take his response.

"Uh, I don't know," Chris stammered. "I don't think we'll be together for long, I guess."

Marielle's jaw dropped. "Don't you still like her?"

"Uh, not really," Chris admitted, "and I think she feels the same way about me."

"Really?" Marielle asked in disbelief. "Then why are you so worried about her?"

Chris sighed. "Don't get me wrong, but I have my reasons."

"Okay."

Chris stared blankly ahead, considering how to tell Marielle the truth. He was interested in Marielle, and that was why he still wanted to pick up Courtney—but how had that transpired? Originally, Courtney had been on his mind. Then, after talking with Marielle, Courtney had merely become an excuse for conversation. What if he was wrong about Marielle? What if she was not the girl from his science class? Would that alter his opinion of her?

"Chris?" Marielle asked, sounding more confused than ever.

"Hi," Chris replied distractedly.

"Did I say something wrong?" Marielle asked apologetically.

"No!" Chris stressed, escaping his daze. "You've been great, really. I was just thinking about what you said. You know, about why I'm going through all this trouble for Courtney."

"Yeah?"

"We just really need to talk things out," Chris stated.

"We've only been together for a month or two, and I don't think either of us will be heartbroken if we're not together tomorrow."

"So you're going to break up with her?" Marielle questioned him, sounding happy with his implication.

"I'm going to talk to her," Chris corrected. "And yeah, probably break it off," he added. "I know you and Court are tight, but could you please not—"

"Don't sweat it, Chris," Marielle interrupted him; "I won't say a thing. Considering the way she's acting, you're way too good for her."

"Really?" Chris asked, thrown off by her unexpected words.

"So what did your cousin say?" Marielle asked.

"Yeah, he'll pick us up," Chris replied absently, dwelling on her last compliment. If Marielle meant what she had said, she obviously thought highly of him. Perhaps was just as intrigued by him as he was by her.

Back at the party, Courtney stood silently beside Bryan and locked her gaze on Jon. It seemed as though everyone's eyes were planted on him, but Courtney's stared deeper. She knew inebriated people often raged, but Jon was completely sober!

A single tear streaked from Alyssa's right eye, but no one crept from his or her spot to comfort her. Seeing Alyssa experience such humiliation made Courtney feel worse about the way she had broken up with Bryan. Jon didn't have to ream Alyssa out publicly. There were hundreds of other ways he could have broken their relationship off. Why had he gone out of his way to hurt her? What had she done to deserve such mortification?

Alyssa's tearful eyes drifted to Cathy. Courtney assumed she was seeking a sign of compassion from her best friend. Cathy wrenched her bloodshot eyes off of Alyssa and glanced at the floor. Courtney watched Alyssa's pain filled expression intensify as she stared disappointedly at Cathy. Alyssa's eyes began traveling from person to person, in search of comfort. Lisa, Leslie, and the other girls had their eyes pasted to the floor. Bryan's eyes were locked on Jon. He appeared disturbed by Jon's performance. Courtney watched a smile widen across Jason's lips, as a short laugh escaped from his mouth.

"This isn't right," Courtney whispered to Bryan as she pushed past him towards Alyssa. Bryan tried to pull Courtney back, but she pressed forward. "Alyssa!" she called, moving between Alyssa and Jon. Alyssa stared helplessly at Courtney. Her face was glazed with confusion, pain, and disgrace. All the eyes in the room immediately locked on Courtney.

"%$&^! The cops are here!" Jason's brother Luke yelled as he ran into the kitchen.

"Crap!" Jason exclaimed, turning his attention to the more serious dilemma. "Everyone get out of my house!" All eyes were torn off of Courtney as chaos erupted throughout the party. The pounding on the front door was barely heard over the uproar of people scrambling towards alternative exits.

"Courtney!" Bryan hollered, pushing towards her frozen body. "Court!" Upon reaching her, he grabbed her hand and pulled her through the crowd and into the foyer.

"What are we doing?" she asked in panic. "We have to get out of here!"

"Just follow me. I know what to do," Bryan urged, opening a closet door. "Get inside," he ordered, entering the overstuffed coat closet.

"Are you crazy?!" Courtney exclaimed, halting at the door.

"They're going to rush in and check the rooms first," Bryan said, pulling her into the closet. "Just be quiet and hide. I know it sounds stupid, but it's worked before."

"Okay," Courtney agreed, layering various coats on top of her. "What if my cell phone rings?"

"Shut it off before it can," Bryan replied, continuing to layer coats and belongings over himself and Courtney.

"I can't see in here," Courtney whispered, searching desperately through her pocketbook.

"Shhh," Bryan hushed, hearing the front door squeak open.

"Police!" an officer shouted, charging into the foyer. From above Courtney's head, she heard the stomping of policemen climbing the twin set of stairs. Blood rushed through her veins, and the hairs on the back of her neck rose. Her eyes widened with fear as an officer paused outside the closet door.

Bryan gripped Courtney's hand tightly and pushed deeper into the walk-in closet. The closet extended completely beneath the set of stairs, forming a makeshift passageway. "I can't see any better than you can, but try to pull as many boxes and big things in front of you as possible," Bryan ordered nervously.

Courtney crawled deeper into the closet with the coats still layered upon her back. The ceiling arched lower as she and Bryan made a sharp right near the end of the closet. Courtney's heart pounded hard against her chest. After crawling as deeply below the stairs as possible, Bryan and Courtney fell flat on their stomachs. Courtney's heartbeat seemed to vibrate on the cold tile floor as she adjusted the coats to cover her petite figure. "They're going to search in here and find us," Courtney trembled.

"No, they're not," Bryan hushed. "Did you see how many people ran upstairs? Did you notice the crowds in the other rooms?"

"Yeah, I guess," Courtney answered faintly.

"Yeah, and there are a lot of drugs and alcohol in the kitchen. The cops are going to be really busy," Bryan added.

"I hope you're right," Courtney said, wishing she had heeded Chris' warning. Chris had proven himself right, and Courtney felt like more of a jerk than ever. She had irrationally flipped out on him, yet he was still trying to help her escape from this hellhole. Even though Courtney had treated Chris terribly, she knew he did not want her to get in trouble. Chris did not have a malicious bone in his well-built body. Suddenly it hit her like a ton of bricks; she was unworthy of his concern or affection.

fourteen

"Hi," Chantal said, welcoming Chris and his cousin into her home.

"Hey," Chris replied distractedly, looking around the foyer. "Where's, uh, Marielle?"

Chantal lowered her eyebrows and glanced suspiciously at Chris. "She's fixing her hair," she responded, observing his nervousness.

"I'm Marc," Chris' cousin introduced himself and set his transparent blue eyes upon Chantal.

"Hi, I'm Chantal," Chantal replied, extending her right hand towards Marc. "But you probably knew that already," she added, studying Marc's features. Marc's eyes might have been a half shade lighter, but they were large and round just like Chris'. Also like Chris, Marc had warm-blonde hair, trimmed short and spiked up. He was well built and most likely a great athlete like his younger cousin. Surely Marc could not have been a day over eighteen.

"So Chris' chic is your friend?" Marc implied with a crooked smile.

"Not really. She's more of Marielle's friend," Chantal replied.

"Oh, the girl Chris is into?" Marc questioned her nonchalantly.

At that moment Marielle paused on the step she had been descending. A bewildered expression coated her face as she glanced from Chris to Marc. She continued to walk down the stairs, slowly and stiffly.

"Yeah, that's right," Chris spoke with his eyes fixed on Marielle.

Chantal's eyes traveled from Marielle to Chris and then to Marc. "Did I miss something?" she asked quietly, struggling to tear her eyes off of Marc's attractive face.

"I tried calling Courtney again," Marielle stated, "but there was still no answer. I don't know what to make of it because she was expecting my call. I hope everything's all right."

"Hey, Marielle," Chris said, looking her up and down. "I, uh, do recognize you from Science."

"Cool," Marielle replied, sending a warm smile in Chris' direction. "I, um, recognize you too."

"We should probably head over to Davids' party before the cops show up," Marc suggested, jiggling his keys.

"Yeah, 'cause they always do," Chris agreed, turning from Marielle to face his cousin.

"Last I heard it was pretty rowdy over there," Marc added. "A lot of my friends are there."

"I hope the cops aren't there already!" Marielle exclaimed with wide eyes. "Maybe that's why Courtney's not answering her phone. Maybe she got arrested!"

"No," Chris shook his head, placing a comforting hand on Marielle's shoulder. "She's smarter than that. Plus, she's with Jon and Bryan; they both know how to outsmart the cops at Jason's house."

Marielle sighed and followed Chris out of Chantal's front door. "I hope you're right."

Jon's body trembled as he climbed the narrow set of stairs leading to Mr. and Mrs. Davids' suite. He couldn't get arrested—not tonight, not after all he'd just been through with Alyssa. He could barely hear the noise from the scrambling party over his pounding heartbeat. Praying that the door ahead of him would be unlocked, he turned the golden doorknob with ease.

Hustling into the suite, Jon locked the door behind him. If the police were going to arrest him, they would have to pick four or five locks. Without turning on a single light, he made his way across the bedroom and into a large bathroom. After locking the bathroom door, he opened another door that led to a dressing room. Jason's house was a maze and nearly impossible to travel through in darkness. Jon felt the wall next to the door in search of the light switch. Because the dressing room was windowless, there was no risk of the police seeing the light from outside. Jon's hand met with the switch as the dressing room illuminated with halogen lighting. Locking the door behind him, he crept further into the shelf-lined room. No one would find him in there, not even Jason. On the other hand, Jason was probably sitting in a police cruiser, claiming none of this was his fault.

As Jon sat down in a plush chair, a picture of Alyssa flashed into his mind. It was amazing how abruptly their relationship had ended; Jon had no regrets, however, except for possibly embarrassing himself. He was confident that their breakup would not be the biggest gossip around school, since half of MLH's students were probably getting arrested.

The cops had shown up at Jason's last party, but Jon, Jason, Chris, Bryan, Cathy, and Alyssa had hid in the dressing room and escaped arrest. If Alyssa did get arrested, Jon knew she would get slammed with community service. After sighting all the drugs and alcohol at the party, the police were sure to run drug tests on everyone they booked. Jon couldn't help but conclude that Alyssa deserved everything she had coming to her.

Jon hoped that Jason would get arrested—just to scare him a little. Partying had begun governing his life. Jason was one of the most intelligent people Jon knew. Despite his frequent drug abuse and painfully teasing nature, Jason was actually a really good friend. Jon hated seeing someone like Jason waste his time chasing after the empty promises of the world. Jason had so much talent and zero desire to do anything productive with it. Jon knew he could say the same thing about himself. He had been walking down a dark path for two years, without a lamp to his feet.

I will lead the blind by ways they have not known, along unfamiliar paths I will guide them; I will turn the darkness into light before them and make the rough places smooth, Jon sighed as he recalled the quote from Isaiah that Chantal had e-mailed him the day before their breakup. Looking back, Jon wished his heart had been fertile enough to absorb the seeds Chantal had tried to plant. By then, his heart had already grown hard. The seeds had been quickly plucked away by the immorality in his life.

"Dude, I can hear the police sirens already," Marc spoke

as he reduced the speed of his red Dodge Dakota to forty-five. "Do you want me to turn down his street? It's coming up."

"Yeah, dude whatever," Chris answered from beside Marielle. He had conveniently offered Chantal shotgun. "I just
can't get arrested, tonight."

"Well, if we just drive down his street, they can't arrest
us," Chantal reasoned.

"Chris has been arrested for stupider stuff," Marc stated,
glancing at Chris in the rear view mirror.

"Oh, my gosh!" Chantal exclaimed, sighting the com-
motion surrounding Jason's house. Sirens wailed from
the numerous cop cars lining his street. Cars with people
scrambling into them were peeling left and right out of
his driveway.

"I didn't know there would be this many people here,"
Marielle said quietly, leaning forward and peering out the
window.

"I don't know about this, little D," Marc said, steering
his truck into a neighboring driveway. "You're out of your
mind if you get out of this truck. The cops will think you
were at the party, and they'll take you in. They know you."

"And then they'll give me a drug test, and I'll be screwed,"
Chris finished, leaning back against his seat. "Why am I
such a loser?"

"Chris," Marielle comforted, placing her hand on his
shoulder, "no cop is going to arrest the mayor's daughter.
Court's fine; I'm sure."

"Let's get out of here," Chris spoke downheartedly, looking at his trembling hands.

"All right," Marc agreed, backing the truck out of the
winding driveway.

"So what's going on?" Chantal asked, turning around to face Marielle and Chris. "Are we going back to your house, Chris, or what?"

Chris remained silent, glancing out the small rectangular window to his left.

"I don't think we should," Marielle reasoned, sending a worried glance in Chris' direction.

Marielle's voice interrupted his daze. "What? Were you just talking to me?" Chris asked.

"Yeah," Chantal replied, flashing him a sympathetic smile.

"Just let me know where I'm dropping you," Marc intervened, without a trace of annoyance in his tone.

"Oh, are you girls coming back to my place?" Chris asked cluelessly.

"Well, we did bring the movie," Marielle implied, meeting Chris' translucent blue eyes.

Chris' lips arched into a smile. "Well then, uh, my place it is."

fifteen

"I can't believe we're getting away with this," Courtney whispered excitedly into Bryan's ear.

"It's getting pretty quiet now," Bryan observed, thrusting a wool pea coat from his legs. "What time is it?"

"I don't know," Courtney answered carelessly, inching closer to Bryan's warm body.

"Where do you think Jon is?"

Courtney shrugged. "He won't get in much trouble if he gets arrested. He is completely sober."

"Yeah," Bryan agreed slowly, "but his mom would kill him."

"Well, whose parents wouldn't? My dad would be so embarrassed!" Courtney admitted.

"Ha! The mayor's daughter at a drug-infested bender," Bryan teased, playing with Courtney's soft hair. "You little rebel."

Courtney turned her head towards Bryan. "Hey," she whispered softly, reaching for Bryan's hand.

"Hey," Bryan returned, taking her hand into his own. Wrapping his other arm around her shoulder, he gazed into her eyes. "I want to kiss you so badly," he admitted, squeezing her hand tightly.

"I'd like that, but—"

"Shhh," Bryan hushed, lightly brushing his lips against hers.

Courtney pulled away. "Bryan, what about Chris?"

"If you want me to stop, I will," Bryan offered. "It will be really hard for me to not try to kiss you again, but whatever you want."

"I just don't want to cheat on Chris," Courtney replied. "It wouldn't be fair."

"Whatever you want, Court," Bryan surrendered willingly, patting the top of her head.

While Courtney and Bryan were escaping detection, Chris was climbing out of his cousin's truck. "Thanks, bro," he said. "Hey, are you sure you don't want to keep Chantal company?"

Marc smirked. "Dude, she's fifteen-years-old!"

"I hate to break it to you, but you're only seventeen, Marky-Marc," Chris laughed, raising his eyebrows in Chantal's direction.

"Na, dude, thanks, but I have plans tonight," Marc replied, glancing at the front steps where Chantal and Marielle were waiting. "I'm going to catch up with Michelle Taylor and them. They avoided Matt and Luke's party, too—smart girls."

"Hey, whatever," Chris said and shrugged.

"Unless you want to come out with us?" Marc suggested. "Robby and Pat are coming out too. They thought you were pretty chill at the concert."

"Dude, I was stoned at the concert," Chris stated, sounding ashamed. "I'm all through with that crap."

"You serious?" Marc asked, raising his eyebrows in surprise.

Chris nodded sternly. "I might be getting pulled up to JV, and I don't want to mess that up. So, since yesterday, no more weed, shrooms, tabs, PKs, alcohol, or anything. I'm all set."

Marc nodded in approval. "Smart," he commended. "If you can stay in line, you'll be better off."

"Yeah, definitely," Chris agreed. "Besides, I want to score it big with Marielle, and she doesn't need a drug-bag boyfriend. I'm trying to quit smoking too. I don't think it suits me very well."

Marc laughed. "I don't think it suits *anyone* well. Pass Chantal my number and tell her to give me a call," he said while revving the Dakota's engine.

"Will do," Chris replied, shutting the passenger side door and backing away from the truck.

"He is hitting on you so badly!" Chantal whispered, raising her eyebrows with interest.

"Na-uh," Marielle denied, although knowing Chantal was right.

"Oh p-lease," Chantal sighed.

"He's Courtney's boyfriend!" Marielle exclaimed loudly.

"Not for long," Chris whispered into Marielle's ear as he snuck up behind her. Marielle shrieked, jumping and reddening with embarrassment. "I'm sorry, did I scare you?" Chris laughed, reaching past Marielle to unlock his front door.

"You have no idea," Marielle responded, catching her

breath as she followed Chris inside.

"Wow, Chris! Your house looks a lot cleaner than I expected," Chantal stated as she entered his home. "Aren't your parents away?"

"Yeah," Chris nodded, leading the girls into his immaculate, country kitchen. "Want something to eat?" he offered, opening his cabinets for any trace of food.

"Looks like the party really cleaned you out, huh?" Chantal commented as she opened the refrigerator.

"Ye-ah," Chris concluded gradually. "We can order take-out if you want?"

"I'm all set," Chantal shrugged as her eyes met with the clock. "Seeing that it's eleven, we should probably start the movie."

Marielle nodded in agreement. "Chantal, how are we getting back to your house?"

A look of concern crept over Chantal's face. "Marc?" she asked, glancing at Chris.

"No," Chris shook his head, "he left to chill with his crew."

"Uh, that's not good," Chantal responded.

"You guys can stay over!" Chris suggested, widening his bright blue eyes.

"I don't think so," Marielle replied, staring at Chris in disbelief.

"No, really!" Chris exclaimed. "Chantal, you've slept over my house before. If your mom let you then, she'll let you now."

"Chris," Chantal said, shaking her head, "we were twelve, and your parents were home. Besides, I slept in Katie's room with ten other girls."

"So, you can sleep in Katie's room, if it will make you

feel better," Chris laughed.

"You're a jerk," Chantal stated flatly, glancing from Chris to Marielle.

Marielle sighed. "If I end up sleeping over, you can consider me grounded for life. I am going to be in trouble when my mom finds out I was in a car tonight, anyway."

"How's she going to find out about that?" Chris challenged, walking behind her.

"She finds out about everything," Marielle replied, rolling her eyes. "It's her 'mother's intuition.' Besides, I actually just got off groundation."

"Will you be grounded when your 'mother's intuition' finds out that I kissed you?" Chris questioned her and turned her around to face him.

"Huh?" Marielle asked, widening her eyes in confusion. Chris lifted Marielle's chin and smiled slightly. Closing his eyes, he pressed his lips softly against hers. Marielle pushed Chris away and stared into his eyes. Slowly, a smile began spreading across her lips. Although there were hundreds of questions racing through her mind, she remained silent.

"Chris, can I use your bathroom?" Chantal asked timidly, darting her eyes from Marielle to Chris.

"The upstairs one is cleaner," Chris hinted and winked at Chantal.

"Oh, hmmm, of course it is," Chantal rolled her eyes and nudged Marielle as she exited the kitchen.

"What was that for?" Marielle asked, warily eyeing Chris.

"Why'd you stop me?" Chris asked, taking a step in her direction.

"You're Courtney's boyfriend!" Marielle exclaimed, reminding herself of how wrong the situation was.

"Honestly, I'd rather be yours," Chris admitted with a shrug and looked directly into her eyes.

Marielle sighed, slumped onto a chair, and rested her arms on the kitchen table. Yesterday, the first day of school, she had spotted Chris in her science class. He had sat towards the back of the lab with Leslie Lucus and Cathy Kagelli. Marielle had only begun watching him because she wanted to look out for Courtney. She had the preconceived notion that Chris was a player, and she expected him to do something to disrespect their relationship. To her surprise, Chris had seemed oblivious to Cathy and Leslie's existence. He took notes during class and appeared genuinely interested in what their teacher was saying. From the way Courtney had described Chris, Marielle had never expected him to care about school. She found herself perplexed by his good behavior and wondering about his character. He did not seem anything like the bad-boy Courtney had described.

Marielle had grown surprisingly jealous of Courtney, while continuing to observe Chris. He had glanced up from his notebook towards the end of class and caught Marielle staring at him. She had immediately turned bright red and dropped her eyes to the floor. He was smiling at her when she looked back up, and she finally realized why girls made such a big deal out of him: he had one of the most beautiful smiles she had ever seen.

Escaping from her daze, Marielle realized she was sitting in Chris' kitchen with him eyeing her expectantly. She could not believe he had interest in her. No one ever had interest in her. Any boy Marielle had liked had always ended up liking Courtney.

It was sweet how concerned Chris had been for Courtney, but what had transformed him into a cheater? Had Marielle been right all along? Was Chris truly the player she had first judged him to be? Did she dare get involved with someone so fickle? She immediately felt bad for even entertaining the idea. The charming, blue-eyed boy staring at her was her best friend's boyfriend. That was a line Marielle never wanted to cross, even in her thoughts.

sixteen

"Court," Bryan whispered, nudging her side. "Court, wake up."

"What?" Courtney yawned, squinting her eyes open. "What time is it?"

"I don't know; I fell asleep," Bryan shrugged, staring admiringly at Courtney.

"Oh my gosh! I was supposed to sleep at Alyssa's!" Courtney recalled, sitting up straight. "Is it morning or still night?"

"We could probably go check," Bryan suggested. "I doubt there are any cops around. Shifts change, and this place cleared out fast."

"I'm still half-asleep," Courtney yawned, thrusting jackets from her lap. "Where are we again?"

"Under Jason's stairs," Bryan answered.

"Oh yeah," she groaned, recalling the events of the evening.

"Did you ever call Chris back?" Bryan wondered.

"He was supposed to call us," Courtney recollected. "I hope he didn't come all the way out here because he couldn't get through to me."

"Would he do that?" Bryan asked.

97

Courtney shrugged.

"I'd do that for you," Bryan stated sincerely.

Courtney smiled. "I believe that. Now, lead me out of this closet."

"Come on," Bryan smiled, grasping Courtney's hand. Moonlight lit the foyer as it shone through the large palladium window. The room appeared empty and the mansion deserted. Still hesitant, Courtney and Bryan crept from the closet and cautiously eyed their surroundings. Bryan tugged on Courtney's left hand and pointed to the kitchen's French doors. Tiptoeing into the kitchen, they found it deserted and piled high with party-debris. "Boy did I pick a bad year to quit smoking," Bryan laughed, picking up a bag of marijuana from the floor. "I wonder why the cops didn't take this?"

"There was so much that maybe they missed it?" Courtney suggested.

"No, it probably wasn't here when they searched the place," Bryan reasoned. "I bet people hid all throughout this house."

"Well, if, uh, that clock's right, then it's 2:30 a.m.," Courtney interrupted, pointing to Jason's microwave. "How did you leave things with your parents?" Bryan asked, leaning against the granite counter. "Were you supposed to check in at a certain time, or what?"

"Uh, no. They were supposed to call me if they needed me," Courtney responded.

"That's funny 'cause your phone was shut off half of the night," Bryan stated, without laughing.

Courtney's eyes widened. "I hope they didn't call Alyssa's parents! That would be bad because my parents didn't know I was leaving her house."

"Do they have Alyssa's number?" Bryan asked.

"Come on, my dad's the mayor!" Courtney exclaimed. "Not to mention that my sister has been dating Alyssa's brother for five years! I think they'll make the Alyssa Kelly-John Kelly connection."

"Well, Alyssa's in jail, so ten to one her parents are down at the police station."

"Ten to one my dad's down at the police station," Courtney sighed, pondering her options. "I should call Chris and try to get us a ride out of here."

"Call him on your cell phone, and I'll use Jay's phone to call Jon," Bryan said, walking over to the wall-mounted telephone. "I know he's either still here or at home 'cause that big bag of weed was his."

"And you know this how?" Courtney questioned him suspiciously.

"Don't look at me like that, Court; I told you I don't smoke anymore," Bryan stressed. "I only know it is Jon's because I saw him bag it with Jason after school. Jay sealed it with a ribbon. Who else ties a quarter with a ribbon?"

"You got me there," Courtney shrugged. "Well, at least we know Jon didn't get arrested. Why did he break up with Alyssa, if he does that crap too?"

"Jon doesn't do drugs," Bryan stated flatly, dialing Jon's number into Jason's phone.

"He wasn't going to deal it, was he?" Courtney asked, her tone clearly stating how disappointed she'd be.

Bryan shook his head from side to side and hung up the phone. "No. Chris gave Jason the money for it on Wednesday night, so Jason gave it to Jon to give to Chris. Sorry to tell you, but your boyfriend has a little bit of a drug problem."

"I don't get why people even bother with drugs," Courtney said. "It's not cool, it's not attractive, and it ruins rela-
tionships. When I started going out with Chris, I had no
idea he was a burnout. And people wonder why I don't
still like him? Maybe he is trying to change, or maybe he is
just distant because of the fight he had with Jason. I honestly don't know. I just want our relationship back, Bry."

Bryan blushed and wrapped his arms around Courtney. "Well, this time I don't want to lose you."

"This time you won't," Courtney whispered into his ear.

In the kitchen of her home, Alyssa stared blankly at her
mother's tear streaked face. Nothing was very clear to her
except how disappointed her mother appeared to be. Why
was she the one crying? Her boyfriend hadn't just publicly
humiliated her. She hadn't just lost the most important person in her life. Yet, Mrs. Kelly was the one shedding tears.

Around the same time, Cathy was inside her own
home, rudely questioning her parents. "Okay, so what, am
I grounded?"

"Boy, is that an understatement!" her father laughed.

"Cathaleen, what made you do all this?" her mother
asked, staring at her in awe.

"Do what, Mom?" Cathy responded in annoyance. "Do I
suddenly not measure up to Chantal? Am I not the perfect
little angel I've led people to believe I am?"

"Cathaleen, we just want to know what has influenced

you," her father pressed. "Whether you see it as wrong or not, getting arrested is not going to please us. Not to mention that you lied and said you were sleeping at Alyssa's."

"I would have slept at Alyssa's after the party if the cops hadn't shown up," Cathy replied without remorse. "So don't even say I lied!"

"You never mentioned a party to us," her mother stated, becoming impatient.

"Oh, so it would have been okay if I had 'mentioned' the party?" Cathy questioned her. "Yeah, I doubt that."

"You can deal with her, Michael. I'm going to bed," Mrs. Kagelli sighed, rising from the kitchen table. "I never thought she and Chantal would grow so far apart."

seventeen

Marielle Kayne —2:30 a.m.

I have told Courtney a countless amount of times that she was crazy to break up with Bryan Sartelli for Chris Dunkin. I was only giving my opinion—you know, trying to be a good best friend. But now, after Courtney finds out that I slept over Chris' house, she is not going to think I was being a good best friend. In fact, she'll probably think I was after her boyfriend the entire time. I mean, why wouldn't she?

Bryan Sartelli —2:30 a.m.

I'm glad Courtney believed me when I told her that I love her. She says she's going to break up with Chris for me, but that could just be a line of bull. I don't think she has a clue what she wants! She's been acting kind of crazy lately. I'm shocked she showed up with Alyssa tonight. The Courtney I dated did not become friends with girls like Alyssa Kelly. I'm guessing Courtney felt uncomfortable at the party, so it's good I took her upstairs to talk. I bet she now understands what I meant when I told her my friends were no good. She always fought me on that. That's cool she didn't cheat on Chris, 'cause I can assume she never cheated on me. Seriously though, Courtney needs to get her priorities straight. I said I'd never let her hurt me again, but I'm a stupid kid.

"Dude, it's almost three in the morning. What the heck are you doing here?!" Chris exclaimed as he opened his front door and let Marc inside his home.

"I didn't feel like driving all the way home," Marc replied, walking into the living room. "Oh hey, you girls are still here?"

"Yeah, we're staying over," Chantal said and smiled brightly.

Marc smirked. "Oh, sorry to interrupt," he said and nudged Chris. Chris rolled his eyes and shook his head, hoping Marc's comment had not embarrassed the girls. Evidently Chantal's parents had an "emergency" arise at home, which caused them to agree to the sleepover. Chris assumed their emergency had something to do with Cathy's attendance at Jason's party.

"How's your girlfriend, little D?" Marc questioned him, sitting down beside Chantal on the love seat.

"You're killin' me, Smalls," Chris replied, shaking his

head and walking over to the sofa where Marielle was sitting. He hesitated slightly before putting his muscular arm around her shoulders. Marielle, who seemed half-asleep, leaned into Chris' chest. Chantal had also seemed tired, until Marc arrived.

"Where's Katie?" Marc asked, taking off his leather sandals.

"Upstairs sleeping," Chris replied. "Unless you woke her up when you peeled onto my street."

"Oh, sorry," Marc apologized, leaning back against the love seat (slightly in Chantal's direction). "I didn't even realize it was so late."

"Where'd you go after you dropped us off?" Chantal questioned him.

Marc shrugged. "I just met up with some friends. It was pretty low key. Plus, I was the DD, so I couldn't drink. What have you guys been up to?" he asked, making eye contact with Chantal.

"We just watched a movie," Chantal said.

"So what's going on with them?" Marc whispered, leaning in closer to Chantal. "Are they together now or something?"

"I'm sure they would be if I wasn't here making the situation awkward."

"Maybe we should leave them alone."

"And go where?"

Marc shrugged. "Wherever you want," he replied vaguely.

"Well, do you mean like in another room or like out somewhere?" Chantal asked.

"It's kind of late, but if you want to go for a drive, we can," Marc offered.

The telephone began ringing loudly, causing everyone to jump in their seats.

"Who is seriously calling this late?" Chris asked, reaching past Marielle for the cordless phone. "Hello?"

"Hi, um, is Chris there?" a hesitant voice responded.

"That's me," Chris replied, trying to recognize the girl's voice.

"Oh, hi," the girl said awkwardly. "It's Courtney."

Chris' heart sank. Courtney was one of the last people he wanted to talk to while sitting beside Marielle. "Oh, hi, Court," he greeted her, watching Marielle's facial expression grow tense. "Where are you?"

"Bryan and I are at Jason's," Courtney told him. "The cops came, but we hid from them in a closet. I was pretty scared, but Bryan knew what to do."

I'm sure he did. "You know, Court, I came looking for you around eleven. The cops were there, so I didn't go inside. Let me ask—why are you calling me now, at two-thirty?"

"Bryan and I sort of fell asleep, but nothing happened, Chris—I swear! Really, you know I would never cheat on you."

"Yeah," Chris said quietly, wishing something had happened so he would have an excuse to break up with her.

"Are you okay?" Courtney asked. "I didn't wake you up, did I?"

"No, Court. You didn't wake any of us up," Chris answered. "Marc, Chantal, Marielle, and I are all wide awake."

"Marielle and Chantal are still with you?" Courtney questioned him with a pang of jealousy evident in her tone. "What are you guys doing?"

"Just chillin'," Chris replied nonchalantly. "They're spending the night."

"Oh," Courtney commented awkwardly.

"Does that bother you?" Chris asked, detecting the uneasiness of her tone.

"No," Courtney said. "It's just random, I guess. I mean, do you even know Marielle?"

Courtney was clueless, and that only made the conversation more uncomfortable for Chris. Was he positive he wanted to break up with her? If he was, should he do it in person or right then on the phone? He had plenty of reasons to break up with her. In fact, she probably was expecting a breakup.

"Court, we need to talk," was all Chris could think to say.

"I know," Courtney agreed, "but can you guys come get us first? I'm just really scared that the cops are going to come back with my dad or something. Would your cousin mind coming out this late?"

eighteen

"Hey, guys," Jon greeted Courtney and Bryan as he entered the kitchen.

"I knew you were still here," Bryan stated, walking away from Courtney, who was still on the phone with Chris.

"Who's she on the phone with?" Jon asked, gesturing towards Courtney as he hopped onto the counter.

"Chris," Bryan replied. "Marc may still be able to pick us up."

"Really?" Jon inquired. "Do you think he'll get me too? I was wondering how I was going to get home. Where do you think Jay is?"

Bryan shrugged. "I have no idea what happened to Jay or anyone else. He probably took off with Luke or Matt. The Davids are pros at getting out of trouble. I'm sure Marc will let us ride in the body of his truck. I just don't know how happy Chris is with Courtney or me."

"Oooh what happened?" Jon sang curiously.

Bryan shrugged.

"Did you score?" Jon whispered, raising his eyebrows in Courtney's direction.

"Courtney's not like that," Bryan replied quickly. "Even

107

when we were together."

"Ah, don't worry about it, guy. I'm not going to be getting much play now either," Jon stated. "I can't believe I broke up with Alyssa tonight. Next week was going to be our thirteen-month anniversary. I really hope I don't regret it."

"Don't worry about that," Bryan stressed. "Alyssa's gone way downhill since you two got together. You know she's not the same girl we used to chill with in seventh grade. Besides, you said last week that you were only staying in the relationship because she's good in bed. I know you want more than that. There are plenty of girls we know who would jump in your pants without a second thought. If you were just looking for sex, you'd stay single and play-around."

"You're right," Jon agreed. "I did pretty well before Alyssa. We didn't even have sex, and I was happier. I was an idiot to let her go."

Bryan nodded in agreement, knowing that Jon was referring to Chantal. He always referred to Chantal. Jon might have caused their relationship to end, but Bryan knew Jon hadn't let her go.

"They're coming," Courtney sang, interrupting Bryan's thoughts. "Chris said only Marc is coming so we can all fit in the truck."

Julianna Camen —3:00 a.m.

It's not just me being insecure when I say that the whole world has forgotten about me. Courtney is out with her new friends, Marielle is sleeping over Chantal Kagelli's, and I am at home with nothing to do. Perhaps I am just feeling sorry for myself, or perhaps I've come to the conclusion that I have no true friends at all.

After Marc and Chantal left for Jason's house, Marielle lay with Chris on the couch; being so close to him brought about a queasy feeling in her stomach. After a bit of resistance, Marc had been able to convince Chantal to accompany him to Jason's. Marielle assumed that Marc had interest in Chantal, but was unable to decipher if it was mutual. Marc was gorgeous, but Chantal was clearly the loyal type—the loyal, taken type, leaving Andy Rosetti without any concern.

Chantal had better morals than anyone else in Marielle's life. After allowing Chris to hit on her so blatantly, Marielle wondered if she appeared malicious to Chantal. After all, Marielle was Courtney's best friend. Alyssa had been Chantal's best friend, until she fell for Jon behind Chantal's back. Jon had been Chantal's boyfriend, until he cheated on her with Alyssa. Marielle swallowed deeply, realizing she was treading in very dangerous water.

"How do you think this is going to go down?" Chris asked, resting the back of his head on his hands and glancing up at the ceiling.

"What?" Marielle questioned him and also glanced at the ceiling.

"Well, you know—us and Courtney," Chris clarified, turning to face Marielle.

"I don't know," Marielle said, holding her gaze on

the ceiling.

"I mean, what are we really?" Chris rambled, setting his eyes on her. "I've made it obvious that I like you, but I have no idea how you feel about me."

Marielle rolled onto her side to face Chris. "I like you in the same way," she admitted hesitantly, "and I would like us to hang out again, but that really isn't an option. You have a girlfriend—my best friend—who is on her way to your house right now. It's not even right for us to talk about liking each other."

Chris nodded and tore his blue eyes off of Marielle. "How about we just play it by ear and see how things go when she gets here?"

"Fine," Marielle agreed, doubting a positive outcome.

Julianna Camen —3:15 a.m.

I wonder what everyone would think if I ran away? Maybe they'd miss me for a few minutes, at least until someone better came along. No, I doubt they'd even notice.

"Hey, Chantal, I didn't expect to see you," Jon greeted her, while climbing into the back seat of Marc's pickup in

Jason's driveway.

"Oh," Chantal replied, sounding more tired than friendly as she avoided eye contact with him.

"Jon, you can put my gym bag on the floor if it will give you guys more room," Marc said.

"Hi, Chantal. Hi, Marc," Bryan called out, following Jon into the truck. "Thanks for picking us up so late."

"We came by earlier but the 5-Os were everywhere," Marc explained.

"That's what Chris said," Courtney stated as she sat down beside Bryan.

"You must be Courtney," Marc said. "I'm Marc, Chris' cousin, and this is Chantal—but you probably know her already."

"No, I don't," Courtney responded in a friendly tone. "Well, it's nice to meet you guys, and thanks for coming both times."

"No problem," Marc shrugged, turning to face Chantal. "We wanted to take a drive anyway."

"Are we all going back to Chris'?" Courtney asked as Marc backed the Dakota out of Jason's driveway.

"My house is on the way, if you want to drop me off," Jon said.

"You live one street over from Chris, right?" Marc recalled.

"Yeah," Jon responded.

"I can drop you off, bro," Marc agreed. "Anyone else?"

"You can bring me home if you want," Courtney said.

"No, not you Courtney; you and Chris need to talk," Marc stated with a short laugh.

Julianna Camen —3:20 a.m.

When I set my mind to something, I usually accomplish it. With my mind set on getting attention, I am going to run away. I'm going to run away from my house and my neighborhood, from Courtney and my parents, and from all the crap I'm going through. Not that running ever solved anything; I am smart enough to realize that.

As the truck approached his house, Jon pointed to a spot where he wanted to be let off. "You can just drop me off at the end of my street. Yeah, right here," he said. "Thanks, dude. I'll give Chris some gas money to give you."

"Don't worry about it," Marc said, leaning his seat forward so Jon could squeeze by.

"Bye, guys," Jon waved, pausing for a second to look at Chantal. She smiled slightly—completely unaware of Jon's single status.

"Later," Marc replied as Jon shut the driver's side door.

Jon watched the truck drive down the main road until it disappeared onto Chris' street. Seeing Chantal always messed with his head. A huge part of him wanted to run to Chris' and find out how she had ended up with Marc. More than anything he wanted an opportunity to discuss their mess of a breakup. He sighed, knowing he did not deserve a moment of Chantal's attention.

Turning left onto his street, Jon heard a faint sound in the distance. *Footsteps maybe? Or a stray dog?* Whatever it was continued to move slowly in his direction. "Hello?" he called into the warm September air. The footsteps halted abruptly. "Who's that?" Jon asked, moving towards the figure that he was unable to recognize. *Surely it is a person,* he thought. *Maybe someone from Jason's party?*

"Who are you?" a timid female voice cried.

Jon continued to move towards the stranger, and then, he halted at a ten-foot distance. Slowly, the girl moved closer to Jon until their distance had diminished to a few feet. Jon studied the stranger in the faint starlight. "Julianna Camen?" he asked, recognizing the girl from his computer class.

"Hi," she said quietly. "You're one of Courtney's new friends, huh?"

"I'm Jon," he introduced himself and stepped closer to Julianna. "We're in the same computer class. You were the only girl I didn't know. What is a smart girl like you doing out here at 3:30 in the morning?"

Julianna shrugged. "It's a really long story. Please excuse me," she said, walking quickly past him.

"Where are you going?" Jon called out after her.

Julianna turned around and stared hesitantly at Jon. "What is it to you?"

"Well maybe I'd like to join you," Jon responded, walking over to her.

"No, you wouldn't want to," Julianna stated, shaking her head. "I'm going nowhere in particular."

"Me either," Jon informed her. "I was supposed to spend the night at my friend's house. I just got dropped off from his party because it got crashed. Do you know Jay Davids?"

Julianna nodded. "He's one of Courtney's new friends."

"Do you keep referring to Courtney Angeletti?"

"Yeah. She and I were best friends for ten years."

Jon lowered his eyebrows in confusion. He would have never correlated Courtney with the timid girl before his eyes. "No way, seriously? What happened with that?" Jon asked, sitting down on the concrete curb.

"I went away this summer with my family; when I came back, she wasn't my friend," Julianna replied and sat down beside Jon. "She broke up with Bryan, the sweetest kid she'd ever gone out with, and started going out with his friend, Chris. That was the end of our friendship."

"Wow, real nice girl," Jon stated sarcastically, realizing how ironic and random the conversation was.

"I guess Courtney thinks she's too popular now for me or Marielle. Now she's friends with Alyssa Kelly and Cathy Kagelli."

"Well here's a news flash for you: Courtney is about to break up with Chris for Bryan; I just broke up with Alyssa; Cathy and Alyssa both got arrested tonight; Marielle is sleeping over Chris'," Jon rambled. "Shall I go on?"

"What?" Julianna exclaimed as if Jon had been speaking gibberish. "Marielle doesn't even know Chris Dunkin!"

"I bet she does now."

"You're making no sense. How did Courtney end up with Bryan?" Julianna asked curiously.

"Now that's a long story," Jon sighed, standing up from the curb. "Let's go for a walk, Julianna," he suggested, helping her to her feet.

———⚜———

"Chantal, can you wait here for a minute?" Marc asked after he dropped off Courtney and Bryan and felt sure that they were out of hearing distance.

Chantal climbed back into his truck. "What's up?"

"Well, I was just wondering if we are going to talk again after tonight?" Marc asked.

"I'd like that," Chantal replied, "but Chris told you that I have a boyfriend, right?"

Marc shook his head. "No, but that's okay. We didn't do anything wrong."

"It doesn't bother you?" Chantal questioned him, raising her eyebrows with surprise.

"Well, sure, it makes me a little sad; but as long as we can be friends I'm cool with it," Marc replied honestly. "You're a great girl. I think your boyfriend's really lucky. Who is he?"

"Andy Rosetti, my grade's class president," Chantal replied. "You might know his older brother, Robby. He's a senior too."

"Oh, yeah, I do," Marc nodded in recognition. "Actually I know Andy too. He's a good kid. Rob came to that concert with Chris and me a few weeks ago. I was actually out with him earlier tonight."

"The Rosetti's are awesome," Chantal stated with a smile. "We'll keep in touch, Marc... and I think we have a very interesting night ahead of us."

nineteen

Chantal Kagelli —4:00 a.m.

His ways are not our ways and His thoughts are not our thoughts. I have no idea how I ended up having such a whirlwind of a night, but I feel like a lot of things are being brought to light. I'm not even going to try to make sense of it. I'm certain that God has His hand in this entire fiasco.

Marielle Kayne —4:00 a.m.

Everything happens for a reason. If Chantal hadn't invited me to sleep over, then I would never be spending the night at Chris'. If Courtney hadn't gone to the party, I would never be spending the night at Chris'. If Chris had gone to the party, I would never be spending the night at his house, and if Courtney wasn't my best friend, I wouldn't feel so guilty.

116

Courtney Angeletti —4:00 a.m.

God works in mysterious ways! Chris and Marielle obviously have something between them. That should get me mad, but it doesn't. I could use my suspicion as an excuse to break up with Chris, or I could just wait a few minutes for him to break up with me. Whatever happens, I'm sure it's all for the best. That would be something if Chris and Marielle got together because of me. I realize I might not be good enough for Chris, but if anyone is, it's Marielle.

Meanwhile, Jon eyed Julianna sympathetically as they strolled along through the still night. "So you are planning to run away?"

Julianna nodded. "Just for a day or so—to get some attention."

"Well, you're already getting my attention," Jon stated.

"Thanks," Julianna blushed.

"You know, Julianna," Jon began, "I don't think running away from Montgomery is going to solve any of your problems. I think what you need to do is face Courtney, face your parents, and face anything else that's bothering you. Stop with all the insecure nonsense and stand up for yourself."

"O-kay," Julianna said slowly.

"No, Julianna. Seriously, I mean what I say," Jon pressed. "You can't see it, but I can see how great your life could be. Just listen to what I'm saying. Courtney is obviously being self-centered. She is wrong, not you; so why should you be the one suffering?"

"Jon, Courtney has a gift called 'popularity,'" Julianna sighed. "If you're friends with her, you obviously know. You have the same gift."

"So, what, her popularity intimidates you?" Jon asked.

"How can I put it? Hmm—Courtney's prideful attitude makes me nauseous," Julianna spat.

"Okay, that works," Jon laughed, surprised by her bold response.

"You're right though. I should confront her," Julianna admitted. "Her and everyone else. I'm the only one who can make myself happy."

"No, now that's where you are wrong," Jon challenged her in a playful tone.

"What do you mean?" Julianna asked, sounding somewhat off-put.

"Well, I think I could make you happy."

Julianna stopped walking for a second, and then continued side by side with Jon.

Jon laughed. "Now you're being the snob!" he exclaimed. "What, you have no response to my offer?"

"Offer?" Julianna questioned him, halting at the sound of his unexpected word choice. "I thought you were challenging me."

Jon shrugged, without pausing next to her. "That too," he admitted.

"So what are you saying?" Julianna asked as she caught

up to him.

"What do you think about making an appearance at Chris' love-triangle sleepover?" Jon offered. "Courtney's there, and I can guarantee she won't be feeling very 'popular.' Chris stayed home with Marielle, instead of going to pick up Courtney. That tells me Courtney is about to get dumped."

"But I thought she wanted to break up with Chris?" Julianna inquired.

"True, but she's totally sweating the idea," Jon said. "I mean, after all, she's pretty crazy."

Julianna laughed.

"So you agree with me now!" Jon exclaimed triumphantly.

"On that note," Julianna nodded, still laughing.

"Oh you *are* coming with me to Chris', Julianna Camen!" Jon sang and spread an amused smirk across his lips.

"Okay," Julianna agreed willingly. "But why are you helping me? You're Courtney's friend. Shouldn't you be defending her?"

Jon shook his head. "When I broke up with Alyssa tonight, Courtney sided with her. All of our other friends knew better than to say a word. Then we got separated for like three hours after the cops showed up. You following me?"

Julianna nodded.

"After the cops left, I met up with Bryan and Court in the kitchen. Courtney was on the phone with Chris, figuring out how she could get home. When she hung up with Chris, she started yelling at me for embarrassing Alyssa. So right now, she's not my favorite person," Jon explained, taking Julianna's hand and leading her onto Chris' street. "So running into you was priceless."

"That's so typical of Courtney," Julianna shook her head and released Jon's hand.

"I thought Courtney was a pretty cool chic, before to-night anyway, so I forced Alyssa to become friends with her," Jon admitted. "All the guys are getting pretty sick of Alyssa and Cathy. I figured because they all like Courtney, they'd like Alyssa more if she hung out with Court. That didn't work, so right now you are my new favorite girl."

"What!" Julianna exclaimed, glaring icily at Jon.

"Well it's a tossup between you and Chantal," Jon added, ignoring the cold stare she'd set upon him.

"Oh, that is enough!" Julianna laughed, stepping away from Jon. "Do you actually think I'm too messed up in the head to see what you're trying to do? Do you think, just because I'm insecure, I'm going to buy into your lines and ignore what I know you're about?" With that Julianna sprinted into the darkness of Chris' street.

"Oh my gosh," Jon sighed, running after her. "That's not what I meant!"

"Courtney, this isn't working," Chris stated, as he shut the door to his bedroom behind him. Courtney nodded in agreement as she sat down at the foot of Chris' bed. "It's not your fault, and I don't think it's mine either. It's just, as boyfriend and girlfriend, we don't mesh very well," Chris reasoned, sitting down beside her. Courtney remained silent, failing to tear her eyes off the floor. "Court, the last thing I want to do is hurt you," Chris expressed his concern, placing a comforting hand on her shoulder. "I mean you're an inspiration to me. Gosh, Court! You're one of my best friends. I hold more respect for you than I do myself. You saved me, Court. You got me to care about my life again. No one else has ever made such an impact on my life. I don't know where I would be if I hadn't met you. You are the best thing that has ever happened to me, Courtney. God blessed me the day you came into my life."

As Courtney glanced up to see Chris' pain filled expression, tears filled her eyes. "Thanks," she mumbled.

"No—thank you," Chris stressed, hugging Courtney tightly. "I care about you a lot, Court, and I want you to always be a part of my life."

"Yeah?" Courtney sobbed, wiping bittersweet tears from the corners of her eyes.

"And I know how you feel about Bryan, but I accept that," Chris added.

"You...you do?" Courtney stammered, sounding more surprised than relieved.

"Yeah. We completely rushed into things. I should have given you more time to get over him, you know, before I swept you off your feet," Chris joked, winking at Courtney. "It was just when I met you, I knew there was something special about you, and I had to find out what. It turns out I was right about something, for once in my messed up life. People probably thought I asked you out because you're beautiful and fun, but, no offense, that wasn't what I was looking for."

Courtney looked surprised. "Wait. What?"

"At Jon's beach party, you remained completely sober around a bunch of drunks and still had a good time. That was the first night I met you, and I was floored by your strength. Being the loser I am, I asked if you wanted to

get high. You simply said, 'No, drugs are against my religious beliefs. They don't interest me.' I remember thinking:
WOW, I want that strength. At that time, I was getting
high or drunk every single day. I felt like I needed to, and
I hated my dependency. That's when I realized what I was
looking for. I wanted an out from my own life-style. When
I saw you, it hit me. You were my inspiration."

Courtney lowered her eyebrows and listened to Chris
intently.

"I knew I couldn't do it alone because I am a very weak
person. The more time I spent with you, the less dependent I felt on drugs. I was doing so much better, until I
agreed to have that party the other night. I completely fell
right back into my old ways. I woke up still drunk, realizing I had blacked out at the party. That's when something
clicked. If I really wanted to straighten out my life, I had
to stay away from my friends completely. That's why I can-
celled the party, and that is what I wanted to talk to you
about at lunch today."

Courtney sat in silence, taking a moment to register
the emotional bomb Chris had just dropped on her. Even
though Chris' words were complimentary, words that
could have enlarged Courtney's ego, she was grieved by his
confession.

"Oh Chris, I am so sorry," she said after a moment of
thought. "I should have heard you out. Instead of being the
inspiration you needed, I fueled the fire of the problem.
There you were trying to escape with me from your friends,
and there I was ditching you for them. Wow. That's. . . . ,"
she put her hands to her tear streaked face and took a deep
breath. She shook her head from side to side, attempting
to grasp the depth of her own shallow behavior. "That's...

geez—that's awful," she finished, letting her tears flow freely.

Chris threw his arms around Courtney. "I wasn't trying to make you upset. I was trying to explain myself to you. I'm sorry, Court."

"No, please do not be sorry," she stressed, pulling away from Chris' embrace. "You just made me realize how lost I've become. You see, steering a straight path isn't easy for any of us. I am so touched by the impact you think I had on your life."

"Good, I want you to be. I want you to realize how much you have done for me," Chris commented.

"Don't you get it though? You went after the wrong person," Courtney said in a soft and sympathetic voice.

"What are you talking about?" Chris laughed. "I went after you. I went after you even though you were dating one of my best friends. Can't you see how selfish I am?"

Courtney smiled. "Like I said, you went after the wrong person. You saw strength in me and said, 'Wow, I want that!' so you went after me. But look at me now. Look at how quickly I let you down. Don't you get it? I am only human; what you saw in me was something much greater. That strength you want can't come from me," she explained. "That strength only comes from God. He is whom you need to go after, not me. I'm so happy you saw that in me. It's just a shame I've backslidden so much and let you down."

Chris lowered his eyebrows and swallowed the lump in his throat that had grown with every word Courtney spoke. *What the heck is she talking about?*

"I'm usually the first one to take credit for something, but even I know my limits. I haven't been to church lately, and I haven't been praying either. I kind of got myself too wrapped up in my social life. What you just said to me made me realize how quickly I lost my strength by being away from God. Do you know I even smoked part of a cigarette today?" Courtney admitted.

Chris shook his head and laughed. "Ha, that'd be a sight to see. That's not the Courtney I know."

Courtney nodded. "I know! Well, Alyssa said you told her I smoked, so I felt like I had to!"

"I never said anything like that. I would never make up a lie about you. Either Cathy made that up, or Alyssa was trying to test you," Chris replied, rolling his eyes.

Courtney shrugged. "It doesn't matter now anyway. I'm over it. But it just goes to show how weak I've become. Saying no to drugs or voicing my beliefs was never hard for me when Christ was the center of my life. I've also grown a hardened heart toward people who were once my close friends," Courtney admitted.

Chris let out a deep breath. "So you're saying what I saw in you was God, and that is what drew me to you?"

Courtney nodded, as a line of tears streamed from each of her eyes. "I think we both misunderstood why we were drawn to each other. It was supernatural."

"I believe in God. I'm Catholic," Chris stated flatly. "How can you go to a party and not even have one drink, and I can't even avoid alcohol in my own home? Why are we so different?"

Courtney smiled. "I saw a huge change in my sister last year, for the better, and I became curious about the cause.

She told me that when she started going to church with her boyfriend, it changed her life. I didn't get it; we had gone to church our whole lives, so what made the difference? She invited me to come and see for myself. That was when I accepted Christ."

Chris felt completely confused. "Like, you got communion?" he asked.

"No," Courtney said and shook her head. "I accepted God's forgiveness."

"Huh? Did you go to confession or something?" Chris asked.

"No, it wasn't anything formal. The gospel was explained in a way I could understand. I finally understood that Jesus had taken my place on the cross. I realized that God is able to forgive me for my sins because Jesus already paid the price for them. That day, I turned my life over to God and asked the Holy Spirit to live inside me and use me for God's purpose. That is what you saw in me.

"I always believed that Jesus was the Son of God, but I never really understood what that meant. I always thought I had to live by the Ten Commandments as best as I could and that when I failed, I had to confess my sins to a priest and just hope someday I would end up in heaven. I never knew much of God's grace. There is no need to say ten Our Fathers and five Hail Mary's in hope that God will forgive us. It's not about anything we do; it's about what He already did for us.

"From the beginning, God required innocent blood to be shed for the remission of sins. That's why the Jews had animal sacrifices in their temple. Then God promised them a new covenant would be made—the Messiah. It was prophesied in the book of Isaiah, and it happened. Jesus shed his blood to cover our sins. His followers are forgiven. That is what the Bible says.

"Do you want to know where my strength came from? Well, a lot of it came from the Holy Spirit living in me," she said slowly, "but some of it came from knowing God loves me. I don't want to hurt Him by sinning against Him. It grieves Him when His children sin because He knows it's only going to cause them pain in the long run.

"Once I let God into my heart, He did wonderful things for me. He had wanted to do them all along." At the sound of her own tender words, she began crying again. "Lately, I haven't done much more than live for myself," she admitted with her chin quivering, "and I am so sorry."

Chris stared at Courtney in disbelief. He couldn't help but think: *What the heck just happened?* Yet, what she said made sense. Hearing her speak about her love for God brought Chris back to the first night he met her. He recalled being undeniably drawn to her, for a reason he couldn't explain. Of course she was beautiful—but he had been around beautiful girls his entire life, so that couldn't have been it. She hadn't been flirtatious either. *Could it really have been God drawing me to her?* He wondered.

Courtney was correct; she had let Chris down. Once his inspiration became less inspiring, he fell right back to where he was before he met her. The thought had never crossed his mind that his desires were of a spiritual nature. Up until this conversation everything in his life seemed trivial. He really had no idea what the Bible said; he had never actually read it. The few times a year he attended church, no one read directly from the Bible. It would be foolish to have an opinion about something he knew nothing about.

Chris believed what Courtney said. What made him believe her, even more than her passion, was the difference he noticed in her from the very start. She made perfect sense; she was only human, and what he saw in her was something far greater. "Court, I'm sorry if dating me pulled you away from God," Chris apologized, putting his head down.

"That's not your fault. I kept myself from going to church and reading His Word. My own selfish desires of my flesh, my pride, my vanity, and my ego got me really lost," she said, wiping the tears from her cheeks.

"So that makes sense. The reason why I had become less attracted to you was spiritual," Chris stated, taking Courtney's words to heart.

"Yeah, most likely," Courtney agreed, taking Chris' hand. "But isn't that cool how attracted to God you were?"

Chris laughed. "Yeah, someone must have been praying for me."

Courtney smiled.

"So, are you going to start going back to church?" Chris asked, gripping Courtney's hand tightly.

Courtney nodded. "Oh yeah. I've seen the person I am without God, and I am pretty ashamed."

Chris had never heard Courtney speak so humbly. The change he saw in her during that conversation alone was enough to make him want God in his life. All along he had gone after the wrong person. "Would it be weird if I came with you to church?" he asked. "Since we just broke up and all?"

"It would be awesome if you came with me to church," Courtney said, smiling warmly.

twenty

"Julianna, will you stop!" Jon pleaded, catching up to the distressed girl.

"I'm sorry, Jon. I'm sorry," Julianna surrendered, slumping to the ground in front of Chris' house.

"Julianna, you're a mess!" Jon exclaimed, looking down at the sobbing girl. He barely knew her, but somehow he felt so involved in her life. She was crazy, stressed to the maximum, and getting on his last nerve. Jon had already ruined one girl's night, and his conscience was not going to allow him to ruin another's. "Let me help you, please."

Julianna continued to sob and tightly grip her knees to her chest. Sighing, Jon did the only thing he could think of: he knelt down and wrapped his arms around her. As he embraced her, his feelings of annoyance transformed into concern. What upset Julianna was greater than the petty problems he and his friends considered life jeopardizing. Julianna's life was more complicated than most. Her friends and family had abandoned her. She needed someone to lean on, someone to listen to her. Jon decided that was where he could come into play. After all, he experienced the pain of a broken home on a daily basis.

128

"You don't understand me," Julianna sobbed. "People actually want to be your friend."

She has a point, Jon concluded, but he knew he had to humble himself. "Julianna, you may think popularity comes easily to me, but I had no idea you felt that way until just now. You see, you have no idea how people view you until you actually sit down and talk with them. You were the only girl who didn't say hi to me in class. Do you know what that made me think?"

Julianna shrugged.

"It made me wonder who you were. I made a mental note to sit near you next class so I could find out. You see, I didn't think you were a loser just because you're not in my group of friends. I knew nothing about you, so how could I have formed an opinion of you? That would have been pretty stupid, and I don't like to think I'm stupid," Jon explained, grabbing hold of Julianna's trembling hand. "You care too much about what other people think of you. If I cared about what people thought of me, I would probably be running away from Montgomery too."

Julianna lowered her eyebrows and pulled her hand out of Jon's grip. "Don't mock me!" she cried defensively.

Jon rolled his eyes. "Julianna, I'm not mocking you; I'm being serious. Let me tell you a little secret about popularity. If you consider someone popular, ten to one they have no idea. People want to be around people who are real. Most likely those people don't even care about popularity. Now, I know there are some people who crave the attention and go to far extremes to fit in. Honestly, all they're doing is robbing themselves of a good time. They should figure out what they enjoy and believe in and do that, instead of trying to please everyone else. Trust me, I know from experience. Everyone is different; that's what makes society function. Don't you think God planned it that way for a reason?"

Julianna raised her eyebrows, eyeing Jon skeptically. "I don't know. I don't really believe God planned anything," she shrugged.

Jon laughed. "Oh okay, so life is just a coincidence?"

"An unfortunate one," Julianna sighed, looking down to her feet.

Jon shook his head. "That's a horrible thing to say. We are so lucky to be alive. The only reason that we are here is because God has a plan for us."

"Oh, so what are you religious or something?" Julianna rebuked, rolling her eyes. "You don't really strike me as the type."

"I have faith, if that's what you mean. Although believing in God is common sense," Jon replied matter-of-factly.

"What do you mean common sense?" Julianna questioned him.

"Well, for one, why am I inside my body and why are you inside yours? Obviously we have souls," Jon stated matter-of-factly.

"I guess," Julianna shrugged, as if she had never considered the possibility.

"It says in the Bible that God created us from dirt, and yes I've read the Bible. Scientists recently discovered that the exact elements that make up the human body, are the same elements found in common dirt. Now science is trying to take credit for discovering something that was written thousands of years ago in the Bible. It just goes to show how stupid people look when they don't take the time to read God's Word," Jon concluded.

"So I look stupid to you?" Julianna asked defensively.

"Well, yeah," Jon nodded. "You're an emotional mess, and you care way too much about what other people think. You're wasting your life caring about things that don't even matter."

"Well, they matter to me," Julianna replied.

"Girl, if you want to feel better you need to wake up. You're like a dark rain cloud. If you want security, you need to get some faith," Jon said.

"Oh, I'm sure that will help," Julianna stated sarcastically and rolled her eyes.

"You've got nothing to lose," Jon stated, standing up in front of Chris' large Colonial home.

Courtney Angeletti—Saturday

I harshly dismissed Julianna from my life, and I failed to be honest with myself. I lied over and over again, trying to convince myself that she had changed and that was why we'd grown apart. It worked for a while; I mean I actually forgot she existed— something I am not proud of. But when I found her this morning, in the emotional state she was in, I found out more about myself than I ever imagined possible:

1) I am no greater than anyone I have compared myself to.

2) What I have thought has made me only shallow and more insecure than the people I have shunned and ridiculed.

3) I have lost sight of everything important.

I grew up inside a bubble; I had the friends I grew up with, my last name that earned me respect, and the gift of charisma. I never had to put in effort to attain any of those things. Suddenly, I was at MLH where there were new faces, new cliques, and new standards. Subconsciously that situation did a number on my self-esteem. When I saw how close Alyssa and Cathy were with a lot of the freshmen guys, I felt threatened—just like I had felt when I saw how pretty Lisa Ankerman was. My desire to remain at the top of the social ladder turned me into a superficial and immoral person. I'm sure everyone could see that—thank God, I now can.

Jon Anderson—the boy I told off for being honest with his feelings—spent the night outside of Chris' house, comforting a girl who meant nothing to him. That should have been me out there, comforting the girl who had been my best friend for a decade. Instead, I had pushed her down to where she was and left her there to rot. And why? Because I felt the need to be accepted by the popular crowd—a crowd made up of people dying to push each other down so they could be on top. When I thought I belonged on their level, I was more than right. I was there already.

Julianna Camen—Saturday

When Courtney came running out of Chris' house

this morning, Chris, Bryan, Marielle, Chantal, and Chris' cousin followed after her. I didn't even look up at any of them; I just kept my eyes glued on Jon. When Courtney and Marielle threw their arms around me, apologizing for causing me pain, I still held my gaze on Jon. I can't believe I spent the night on the street, crying my eyes out in his arms. He must think that I have serious problems! I, on the other hand, think Jon's the sweetest kid I've ever met. Despite how many friends he has, I think I've seen a side of him the others haven't. He was sensitive, understanding, and patient with me. He gave me the support I needed to be honest with my feelings. Jon Anderson made me happy, something I was incapable of doing. I'm trying to decide whether or not I should let him know this. But I know one thing: I'm through with running. I've received something greater than attention. My eyes have been opened to something I never before considered. It's possible my life may have a purpose.

Jon Anderson—Saturday

I never fell asleep last night; instead, I found something in myself. What I found was the faith in me that I had begun to question still existed. Chantal and I met at church, we hung out at church, and we centered our relationship on our mutual Christian values. I can't complain—our relationship was amazing. To this day I am shocked she broke up with me, but at the same time I can understand where she was coming from. I admit that I started doing things I had always been against. My friends started partying, and I felt the need to keep up with them. I didn't want to lose my friends! The more I partied, the more I lost sight of what was important to me. Then, I eventually lost Chantal. Sadly, I haven't been to church since. So I ask myself, where has my new life gotten me?

My friends—you know, the ones I sacrificed my morals in order to keep—I don't even like them anymore. I was bored out of my mind at Jason's party last night. Anyone with eyes or ears could tell you I was incredibly annoyed. I've done my share of partying, but it's just not for me. Not the way they party. Nothing positive comes from it. It's so frustrating to see people I care about flushing their lives down the toilet—like Alyssa, for example, whom I've known for years. Honestly, she has good intentions. I see her giving into peer pressure and falling apart right in front of me as a result. Last night, I completely snapped. I couldn't take it anymore! I can't live that life any longer, not after comparing it to how great my life once was. That was why I had to give Julianna tough love. She probably wouldn't believe me if I told her I had felt the same way as her two years ago. That was the epiphany I had when I was talking to her last night. It wasn't worth it! None of it was. I should never have sacrificed my own beliefs to fit in. I was much happier being in a relationship with Chantal that was centered on our faith.

Staying up all night with Julianna was the most unselfish thing I have done in a long time. Funny though, I think I got more in return than I gave out. I don't want to see her make the same mistakes I did. When you feel that alone and hollow, there is only one person who can fill you. I think you know by now whom I'm talking about. His name is Jesus Christ, and He laid down His life for you.

twenty-one

"Oh look! It's the girl who changes boyfriends every week!" Cathy exclaimed Monday morning, glaring icily at Courtney in the freshmen locker hall. Alyssa appeared beside Cathy and gazed disapprovingly at Courtney.

"Just ignore them, Court," Jon stated loudly as he stood between Courtney and Julianna.

"Alyssa, do you have a problem with me too?" Courtney asked, raising her eyebrows in disbelief. "That would be odd seeing that I was the only one who stuck up for you at Jay's."

"Courtney, I don't know what you're talking about," Alyssa replied coldly. "My memory of Friday night is as blurry as our friendship. You know, like it doesn't exist."

"Fine," Courtney shrugged, smiling as she turned to walk away.

Alyssa scowled. "Seriously, just like that?" she called loudly down the corridor.

Courtney paused for a moment and then continued walking. *Yup. Just like that,* she thought.

Marielle Kayne—Monday Night

Finally things have returned to normal between Court, Julie, and me. Chantal really fits in well with us, and her boyfriend Andy seems really nice. Over one weekend, I gained an entire group of friends. I think I'm going to like high school!

"I thought I might find you here," Jon sang, greeting Julianna at his locker Tuesday morning.

Julianna shrugged. "Well, I figured if I stood here long enough, you or Court would show up."

"Well whose locker are you waiting at? Courtney's or mine?" Jon questioned her as he turned his combination lock.

"Yours," Julianna replied with a twinkle in her blue eyes.

"That's what I like to hear," Jon said with a laugh, as he placed his history book on the top shelf of his locker. "So what's up?"

"Marielle, Chris, Chantal, and Andy are doubling for the dance next Friday. So Courtney and Bryan want us to go with them. I guess they figured we're going together or something. I don't know what made them think that."

"Me," Jon admitted as he turned to face Julianna. "I told them yesterday that I wanted to ask you to the dance, and they suggested that we all go together. They must have thought I had already asked you."

"So you really want to take me to the dance?" Julianna inquired, staring at Jon in disbelief.

Jon nodded. "As long as you make a habit of hanging out with me more often," he said and smirked.

With a bashful smile, Julianna blushed deeply. "I can do that," she replied, incapable of wrenching her eyes off of Jon.

Chris Dunkin

So, it was an eventful first week of school. I can't honestly guess many of the events will mean anything to me five years from now, but I know the friendships will. If you had asked me a year ago, I probably wouldn't have been able to confidently say that.

It was nice to see Jon's sights on a nice girl like Julianna. Actually it was nice to see Julianna bring out the caring side of Jon. I hadn't seen that since he and Chantal dated. Then again Chantal always had a way of bringing the best out in everyone.

I saw Chantal when I went to church that first time with Courtney. She was there with her parents, her little sister, and Andy. She was shocked to see me! I told her briefly what had happened between Courtney and me during our breakup. She smiled and said God had answered her prayers. I found out that she had been praying all year that God would find a way to reach me. I knew someone must have been praying for me, and I love Chantal for being that person. I think her prayers got me to Courtney, Courtney got me to church, and church got me to God. I don't just mean church taught me about God; I mean in church I got to know Him through His Son.

It was there at the altar, at the end of service on that first Sunday, that I got the strength I needed to straighten out my life. The ironic thing is that I didn't pray for strength specifically—I repented. I put my faith in Jesus Christ. It's an experience that words cannot explain to anyone, but it is amazing. It changed my life. Actually it gave me life. I think we are all born dead and the way we receive life is through rebirth. You see, I died to myself; so now through Christ I have eternal life. Accepting Jesus Christ as my Savior is the one thing I know I will remember about my first week of high school for the remaining years of my life. I got saved from myself, saved from hell, and saved from an empty, futile life-style. Salvation is the best gift anyone could possibly receive.

After that Sunday my desires began to change. I didn't even have to ask God to take them out of my heart; He just did it on His own. That was five months ago. I've been sober ever since.

More Titles In
The Montgomery Lake High Book Series

Montgomery Lake High #2: When Darkness Tries to Hide
As the skies grow darker and darker over Montgomery Lake
High, not everyone takes the severe storm warning seriously.
A day later, Andy Rosetti—the popular class president—is in
a coma, and his classmate Jason Davids feels responsible
for the tragedy. As Andy's friends and family cope with the
aftermath of the storm, Jason and his friends set out on a
quest to save Andy's life. Stopping at nothing, Jason begins
to see that there are forces stronger than nature at work in
Montgomery—and more than one life in need of saving.

Montgomery Lake High #3: The Battle for Innocence
Within a dimly lit hospital room, Chantal Kagelli peers at
her boyfriend Andy's blank face. It has been one month
since he slipped into a coma—one month since she last
heard his voice. Chantal begins reflecting on their journey,
which began two years prior in seventh grade. The Battle
for Innocence flashes back to that pivotal year when the
characters of Montgomery Lake High were first introduced
to the temptations, peer pressures, and internal-struggles
associated with adolescence.

The Aftermath: Jason's Story
For the past two years, Jason Davids has lived a charmed
life. Blessed with good looks, a popular girlfriend, quick wit,
and a wealthy family, Jason has everything he could want–
but everything is not enough. There is emptiness–something
unsettled in his soul. Partying, drugs, sex, and alcohol provide

temporary relief, but the haunting emptiness always returns once he is sober. He can't stand being sober. When a tornado strikes his town, Jason's drug dependency puts one of his classmates, Andy Rosetti, in danger. After Andy is taken away on a stretcher, the guilt and regret that Jason feels lead him to a paradoxical place of darkness and illumination. There is more than one life at stake in Montgomery.

The Forces Within: Andy's Story
Last month, when a tornado wreaked havoc on my hometown, I suffered a severe head trauma. I have since experienced something much more disturbing. During my recovery celebration, I came face to face with a force more powerful than any weather phenomenon, something darker than I ever dared to imagine.

Twice this past month, I woke up in a world that I did not recognize. I heard things that didn't align with my memories; things that made me question my identity, my beliefs, and my own thoughts. I still cannot fully comprehend what happened to me or distinguish reality from illusion.

Am I, perhaps, discerning an additional dimension of life that I was too blind – too jaded, too scared – to see before? Could the forces within these two worlds exist as one? I'm determined to solve this mystery and gain all of the insight that I can from the haunting enigma that has recently become my life. – Andy

The Forces Within follows Andy Rosetti and his friends' chilling adventure at Fallen Lake. Could Andy be stuck between two worlds, or have his eyes been opened to see a deeper reality?

CPSIA information can be obtained
at www.ICGtesting.com
Printed in the USA
FFOW02n1811041216
29890FF